Seducing the
Rain God

Seducing the Rain God

Translated from Bishnupriya Manipuri by
Ramlal Sinha

A collection of short stories from the North-East
by
Smriti Kumar Sinha

NIYOGI
BOOKS

Published by

NIYOGI BOOKS

D-78, Okhla Industrial Area, Phase-I
New Delhi-110 020, INDIA
Tel: 91-11-26816301, 49327000
Fax: 91-11-26810483, 26813830
email: niyogibooks@gmail.com
website: www.niyogibooksindia.com

Text © Smriti Kumar Sinha
Translation © Ramlal Sinha

Editor: Mohua Mitra
Cover Design: Ritu Topa
Layout: Sarojini Gosain

ISBN: 978-93-83098-79-8
Year of Publication: 2015

Printed at: Niyogi Offset Pvt. Ltd., New Delhi, India

CONTENTS

AUTHOR'S NOTE

I feel privileged that I'm born and bred in a family humbly devoted to art, culture and literature. Naturally, I'm a great admirer of any creative expression in these domains from childhood. But I pursued science, particularly physics, as a course of my study; and then migrated to computer science. Mathematics is my preferred language. I feel more privileged today to enjoy both the domains of arts and science.

I have been an ardent reader of literature from childhood, but never dreamed of being a poet or a writer. My homecoming happened out of a social need. During my student days in G.C. College, Silchar, one fine morning I was depressed over the plight of the literature of my mother tongue—Bishnupriya Manipuri, an endangered language, struggling to survive. The corpus of poetry was matured enough. Fiction, however, was still trying to structure itself. I decided firmly to write novels and short stories only in my mother tongue. The main aim was to revitalise the moribund language, enhancing its prestige by producing high quality literature at par with other Indian regional literature. The target audience at that point of time was a very small group of readers among the speakers of the language.

Indian literature, I believe, is not the sum total of the works published only in English, Hindi and other major Indian languages. This partial sum provides only a partial view of the vast literature and culture of India with more than 1600 languages and dialects. Apart from its communicative role, a language works as a vital social identity. Literary works in endangered dialects and minor languages of India are also equally important components of Indian literature. Publication and publicity of quality works in such minor and endangered languages will be the true and ultimate recognition of creative writing from all corners of India. This collection comprises English translations of fourteen of my short stories. I sincerely hope it will get a wider audience in India and abroad. If the esteemed readers – especially the younger generation – find the stories interesting, it will be my ultimate reward and a step ahead in the efforts for revitalising and boosting the Bishnupriya Manipuri language.

– Smriti Kumar Sinha
14 July 2014

TRANSLATOR'S NOTE

*T*he period between late 20th and early 21st century witnessed the emergence of the ethnic press of the Bishnupriya Manipuri community, creating a classic alternative media. It was a significant step forward after the launch of *Jagaran* – a trilingual magazine first published in 1925 in Bishnupriya Manipuri, Bengali and English – in undivided Sylhet district of Assam.

In a bid to fight rampant language cannibalism, various Bishnupriya Manipuri organisations, social activists and litterateurs have been striving to put their ethnic language and literature on a sound footing and subsequently on the world map. Though *Jagaran* did not last long, it did lay the foundation of the movement for the revival of this endangered language and its literature and bringing it to the pan-Indian forefront. The flame lit by *Jagaran* has been kept alive by little magazines; Bishnupriya Manipuri writers and social activists are still burning their midnight oil for the revival of the language and literature as a labour of love.

The need of the hour is to build bridges through translations and connect the thoughts of the writers of this community hailing from landlocked North-East with a wider global audience. The present collection has fourteen short stories originally written in Bishnupriya Manipuri by Prof. Smriti Kumar Sinha and a few of them have been published by Pouri International, Bangladesh.

As a short story writer, Prof. Sinha – who has been writing short stories for over three decades – reveals a strong voice with a distinct timbre. His style of narrative is a vivid portrayal of life. The original Bishnupriya Manipuri versions of these stories have been published in three collections and in some magazines. The translations have been created from a revised version of the original stories and have undergone careful editing and revision at the publisher's end to bring in greater lucidity and aesthetic conformity in the prose without disturbing the unique essence of the original stories, the events, the subtle but significant cultural references and the characters.

– Ramlal Sinha
24 July 2014

FLOWERS WITHOUT FRAGRANCE

*G*okul stood in their banana grove before taking a bath—a habit he had been in for the past few months. With eyes set on a bunch of bananas, he had his head resting against his shoulder. He was licking his dry lips. His eyes suddenly lit up with joy and he rushed home, clapping. Running to his elder sister Kusum he whispered, "Iche[1], the bunch of bananas has started ripening."

"Is that so?" Kusum asked, widening her eyes in excitement. He caught hold of her by the wrist and pulled her quickly to the banana grove. Pointing his index at a banana, Gokul exclaimed with his baby lisp, "Look! It's lellow!"

"Oh, yes!" Kusum replied. "But how did you spot it? It's almost hidden!" Without responding to her, Gokul kept gazing at the banana. He gulped saliva, nay, the ripe banana as though that had failed to withstand his piercing gaze and had fallen right into his mouth.

Kusum saw her father coming in through the main gate. "Eiga[2] is coming," she told Gokul.

"Where's he?" Reluctantly Gokul moved his eyes from the bunch of bananas. They ran towards their father, scrambling to

---

1 Iche: A salutation to an elder sister.
2 Eiga: A salutation to father in royal families.

be the first to inform their father of the ripe banana. Since Kusum outpaced Gokul, he tricked her and screamed the message across to his father before actually reaching him. "Eiga!" he gushed. "The banana bunch has started ripening!"

Golapsena Rajkumar held his son and daughter and hid a wry smile. The two siblings almost fell over each other, excitedly giving him the minutest details of the bananas—in which cluster and how many, their colour, on which side the bunch leaned, and the like.

Golapsena Rajkumar. Rajkumar, a prince! He himself was ignorant of where exactly his forefathers had been kings and how big their kingdom was. He, however, had witnessed what kind of a 'king' his father had been. He too had lived like a prince.

Sitting on a *fita*[3] day in, day out, his father used to puff on the hookah. Not to speak of any agricultural activity, he had refrained from doing any work to eke out a living. Strangely enough, the kitchen fire kept burning round the clock. Golapsena was in the dark about where the money came from. But after the discovery of the cash cow – his royal lineage and the perks that came with its hangover – he was simply dumbstruck.

After leading a lavish life, his father breathed his last with the hubble-bubble in his hand. His mother too followed suit after hearing the patter of tiny feet – her grand daughter's – but her dream of seeing the girl's wedding remained unfulfilled. Erroneously left behind, Golapsena staggered under the burden of the family that his parents had built and left behind. The only fortune he had inherited from his extravagant father was half of their old residential plot and the ruinous title—Rajkumar! He would have had a respite from penury had he not inherited this title that prevented its holders from ploughing the fields

---

3 *Fita*: A royal seat woven with cotton thread.

and working as daily-wage earners. He was a victim of the last vestiges of royalty—the title 'Rajkumar'.

In order to strike a balance between the splendid aura of his inherited regality and livelihood, he had been in army recruitment rallies, but to no avail. The job demanded educational qualifications, not royal descent and high breed. Taking all aspects into consideration, he started a business venture with a grocery shop. The venture was in the red danger zone within five months by virtue of a pack of credit-unworthy customers. He proved the veracity of the popular belief—two things that can't last long among the Bishnupriya Manipuri people are shops and social organisations.

For around eight years, Golapsena had been bearing the brunt of penury but he had none to help him out. With repeated pleas from his wife, Kamalini, an emotional Golapsena today approached *muktiar*[4] Baladev, and said: "Khura[5], I can't carry this burden any more. You can bail me out from this gutter. You just give me three *bighas*[6] of arable land. I've no way out but to be a sharecropper, else my kids will starve."

"What! Want to be a sharecropper? You mean cultivation? What's wrong with you?" a stunned Baladev questioned Golapsena.

"Yes, I exactly mean that. I feel as though I'm on the threshold of a new life. I've to get out of this royal hangover. You see, starvation and death continue to haunt my children," a determined Golapsena replied.

"What rubbish! A royal scion paired with the shaft of a plough! Strange bedfellows! How dare you set such a precedence? Should you break free of the sacred royal cow?"

---

4 *Muktiar*: A village arbitrator.
5 Khura: Uncle; reverential address for a village elder.
6 *Bigha*: A measure of land.

"You are right, Khura, but don't you see, how I've to bear the brunt of this tradition?" Golapsena rued.

"Krishna, Krishna. It's the inscrutable ways of God. You can't make both ends meet today. With God's grace, you may have more than enough tomorrow. Frolicsome God is playing a game with you. You're in distress. Aren't we all?" an emphatic Baladev tried to reason.

"It's not my wish, but I've no way out," said Golapsena.

"*No way out* is what I can't agree with," said Baladev with much annoyance. "Your father Gontagiri and your grandpa Senarigiri could live a lavish life without having seen the paddy field," he added. "Why can't you?"

"I'm a flower without fragrance. I'm reduced to rags. I lack the wherewithal to keep the kitchen fires burning tomorrow," revealed Golapsena. That left Baladev to pretend as though he hadn't heard what the visitor had uttered. He kept on delivering an uninterrupted lecture. "The entire Bishnupriya Manipuri community is sliding down and hitting rock bottom. Even the Brahmins drink tea with non-Manipuris and *nahumwallas*[7]; the Rajkumars are the only ones who have kept the community still illuminated. If you too take to ploughing, then God help us! How can we hold our heads high before others?" Baladev rued.

"Royal scions like me are flowers without fragrance. It's okay. I won't take to ploughing, but please have the patience to listen to me. Forget about us, but I can't think of my children starving," said Golapsena. He appealed to Baladev: "Khura, would you kindly lend me a few *kathis*[8] of paddy for the sake of the kids? I will pay you back in the forthcoming harvesting season."

---

7 *Nahumwallas*: Those wearing skull caps.

8 *Kathi*: A traditional Manipuri bamboo bowl for measuring rice.

Baladev lowered his tone, and said: "*Giri*! Why as loan? You're worthy to get free of cost. However, the yield of paddy this year just hasn't measured up. This apart, we have a *divas*[10] on Sunday next."

"Oh! I see," Golapsena said hanging his head down to hide his blushes, and left.

*

HOLDING his two kids by their hands, Golapsena came back to his courtyard. Kamalini had been waiting in hope, holding on to a post in the verandah. Golapsena glanced at her and then dropped his sunken eyes. The nutritious diet of his childhood had left its glow on his cheeks but the eyes...Kamalini could read his face right. Drawing a deep sigh, she let go of the post. "Go and take a bath with your Eiga. I'm serving lunch," she told Kusum and Gokul.

After taking a bath, Golapsena sat on a *chakchafal*[11]. While serving food, Kamalini asked him: "What's the outcome of meeting Baladev-khura?"

"Nothing," came the curt reply, devoid of any frills.

Keeping silent for a while, Kamalini said anxiously: "What to do? Not a single grain is left for tomorrow."

"On way back home, I dropped in at Gaurhari grandpa's shop," Golapsena said, raising his head a little.

"Yet again?" she choked.

"What else can I do? I ..." Golapsena failed to complete his sentence as both Kusum and Gokul entered. Looking at the plates, Kusum said: "Ima, you have cooked arum again."

9 Giri: Your Highness.
10 *Divas*: A religious service for the devotees of Lord Vishnu.
11 *Chakchafal*: A flat low wooden stool used for sitting during mealtimes.

"Yes, have it. It's nutritious. Rich in vitamins...," Kamalini told Kusum in an appeasing tune.

"In the name of vitamins, you keep feeding us arum with only a little rice everyday. I won't have this yucky food," Kusum said, and stood up defiantly, rubbing her eyes. Her copycat Gokul followed suit.

"I'll serve you more rice if you need," Kamalini said, and made Kusum sit down. Imitating his sister, Gokul too sat down. After a while, Kusum said: "Ima, give me more rice." Gokul made no delay in following suit.

Kamalini took out a lump of rice from the pot, and distributed it between Kusum and Gokul. She had kept that lump for herself. Golapsena was about to add some more rice to the curry but stopped short of doing so, after noticing the empty pot, Kamalini and the two kids. He held the water glass and stood up leaving half the rice on his plate.

"What happened?" a stunned Kamalini asked him.

"Something is wrong with my stomach. I don't wish to eat any more," he said, and went out. Kamalini understood. She looked at him, rubbed her eyes with the hem of her shawl, and took the plate.

*

Lying in bed, Golapsena glanced at Kamalini, who was busy eating his leftover rice. He heaved a deep sigh, noting her bare wrists, ears and her empty neck. The daughter of the famous scholar Dhana Pandit! Hers was a classic tale of 'riches to rags' after her marriage. He could hardly offer her bangles or earrings. She had to confront the first wave of penury in the family. Weaving day in and day out, she was responsible for earning a living for her family. Despite all that, she was never proud of her contribution to the family. For about a month, her wings had been clipped. They had no money to buy yarn and other weaving materials. All wasn't lost yet. She continued to badger him into taking up agriculture as his profession. She put forth arguments to prod Golapsena into action, "King Janaka was a cultivator. Is our royalty greater than that of Janaka?"

"A convincing logic, indeed, but..." Golapsena's thoughts wandered drowsily into a snatch of sleep. In the afternoon, he cut the bunch of bananas and stored it inside the empty granary.

*

It was Govardhan Puja the next day. Since the early hours of dawn, the village children had been hopping from pond to pond, scooping out damp clay. Kusum and Gokul were also busy making clay idols in the courtyard. While Kusum made a buffalo, Gokul took two bamboo branches, bound them with a thread and a stick as a plough shaft. He also made a clay idol and attached it with the shaft depicting the picture of a man tiling the fields. The two siblings went to the community *mandap*[12] with their clay models. In order to have some fun, Baladev and two other muktiars asked Gokul: "Oh my dear boy! Who's this man tilling the field?"

Looking at the model, his creation, Gokul said with a sense of satisfaction, "It's me."

The three muktiars stood stunned.

Golapsena took out the bunch of bananas and sat on the verandah. Since the unplucked bunch had started ripening, the top two tiers had ripened on their own.

---

12 *Mandap*: A makeshift canvas enclosure decorated with lights and buntings where the idol is placed and worshipped.

"Make sure that Kusum and Gokul don't see the bunch while being taken to the market," Kamalini cautioned Golapsena. Rubbing her face with a bandanna, she reminded Golapsena again: "It's better to rush now. There'll be hell to pay if Kusum and ..."

"Oh, yes," Golapsena stood up slowly.

"If you can, keep a cluster of bananas for the kids," Kamalini requested her husband.

"How can that be?" Golapsena said, while stepping down to the courtyard and heaving up the bunch of bananas. "After a hard bargain, Gaurhari grandpa had agreed to buy the entire bunch at rupees six. If I put a cluster away for the children, how can I buy rice and bring it home?" he argued.

Wham! Kusum and Gokul tore in, shouting. Hastily, they made it to the courtyard through two horizontal bars of the bamboo gate. Kusum held on to the bunch of bananas from behind, and said: "No Eiga, please, don't take it. Not again."

A silent Gokul simply held on to the bunch with Kusum, as hard as he could. Choked with tears, Kamalini covered her face with the shawl and ran into the house.

Golapsena clenched his teeth and turned back.

"Hell-bent on eating bananas! Leave it! I say, leave it!" Golapsena tried to wrench it away. The two siblings put in an even greater effort. A flared-up Golapsena landed a tight slap each on their tender cheeks. He snatched the bunch from their clutch. Knowing not where and how to hide his hand, the poor father rushed towards the gate, his hand waggling by his side. His heartache soon pervaded his entire being, but he continued to walk on.

With tears streaming down their cheeks, Kusum and Gokul stood still, looking at their father fading into invisibility.

A PAGE FROM THE MAHABHARATA

*S*unday morning. Polishing his spectacles to an immaculate shine, Narendra sat in front of the television in the drawing room.

"Has it started?" His wife, Surabala threw him an anxious query from the kitchen.

"No."

Surabala was busy preparing breakfast. With the TV serial about to start, she was in a tearing hurry.

"Hasn't it started yet?" she asked him again.

"No, not yet. I'll call you. The signature tune will also let you know," assured Narendra.

At that very moment, a scooter stopped in front of their gate. Narendra looked out through the window.

"Hey, do you hear me? Sunanda and Surendra have come!" He rushed to open the door.

"What a pleasant surprise! Welcome, welcome. I can hardly believe that you have come," said Narendra. Surabala quickly added two more cups of water in the kettle, for tea. She hurriedly rustled up a couple of omelettes as well.

"Has it started?" Surendra anxiously asked Narendra as he set foot in the verandah.

"About to. We too are waiting for it," assured Narendra.

While Surendra sat in the drawing room, Sunanda went straight to the kitchen to meet Surabala. After a while, the two women came out with tea and snacks to the drawing room.

"Have you lost your way and ended up here?" Surabala took a dig at Surendra. Surendra replied with a smile: "Oh no, it's not like that. We had been planning, you know. We planned to catch a glimpse of your new house and, while at it, to enjoy the *Mahabharata* serial together."

"It's nice that you have come," said Narendra.

"Perhaps the birth of Krishna will be screened today."

"How can that be? Just the fourth child was born in the last episode, and Krishna was the eighth."

Sunanda however, had her eyes set on a bonsai banyan tree near the TV. She studied it keenly, and asked: "Where have you brought this bonsai from?"

"From the horticulture firm in Zoo Road."

"Beautiful! With prop roots coming down, it looks like the old gigantic one near the Mahabhairav temple."

They all burst into laughter. The sky-high, royal, gorgeous and long-living banyan tree had been dwarfed into a comic caricature. Its only challenge lay in reaching the TV on the stand—thanks to those who had cut its roots to stop its growth.

Soon the day's episode of the *Mahabharata* began. The room wore a mantle of silence. At first, a recap of the last episode was telecast ... Daibaki[13] gave birth to her fourth baby in the prison. She made every possible effort not to let the guards on duty learn of the arrival of the newborn. However, a spying guard came to know of the infant and passed the message on to King Kangsh late at night. The day's episode started....

A beam of light from the rising sun illuminated a corner of the prison cell. Daibaki, who had to pass a sleepless night, was taken aback by the light. Vasudeva, on the other hand, kept looking at

13 Daibaki: Devaki, Krishna's biological mother.

the baby in bewilderment. A restless Daibaki was on a desperate lookout for a safe hideout, but to no avail. The guards were about to reach her cell. She was crestfallen when she thought of the fate of her baby when her brother Kangsh would...

"Let's do something. It's morning. Where can we hide the baby?" Daibaki asked, and brought Vasudeva back to his senses. He kept looking at her and the newborn. Raising his chained hands up, a helpless Vasudeva kept praying at the beam of sunlight. The oracle went that the eighth son of Daibaki would be their saviour. Oracles always came true, but it's all the same to parents—the first or the eighth. "Oh God! What an ordeal is this!" Vasudeva rued, and kept gazing at the sky, at the fragment of blue which peeped in through a small hole.

"King of Kings, His Highness, King of Mathura, Maharaj Kangsh is c-o-m-i-n-g ..." a royal guard sounded an alert. A frenetic Daibaki kept running from one corner to the other to hide the baby. Her chained legs were bleeding profusely. At last she lay on her side and started breastfeeding the baby. She pretended to be oblivious of the arrival of Kangsh, who entered the room and said: "Daibaki, hand over the baby."

"Baby? What baby? There isn't any."

"Don't hide it. I've come with a confirmed tip-off."

"I'm bowing down to you, pleading you to spare the life of an innocent infant," she said. Kangsh was bewildered, looking at his most loving sister. But he soon came to his senses, and thought, "That can't be. For my life, the death of Daibaki's babies is a must. Defending oneself is no sin." He laughed in her face, and took away the infant from her lap, raised it up and smashed it against the wall. Fresh blood dripped down the wall, making the sight a gory one...

*

A commercial break followed. The television's volume was low. A pin-drop silence enveloped the drawing room. Only the 'tick-tock-tick-tock' monotone of the wall clock continued.

"Detestable!" Sunanda broke the silence, indignantly.

"No character in the *Mahabharata* is as sadistic as that of Kangsh," Surabala remarked.

A commercial advertisement was on the screen. Silently the advertisement showed the preparation of tasty chocolates from milk collected by women's cooperatives in Gujarat. A success story! The ad, however, stopped short of addressing the plight of the calves, deprived of mothers' milk.

"A sadist, you know," taking a piece of the omelette, Narendra continued. "It's the height of cruelty. For the sake of his own life, so many innocents were slaughtered. Horrible! The director has done the job well, symbolically showing patches of blood on the wall...a balanced shot."

"Wait, wait. The omelette is delicious. The taste isn't as insipid as that of the regular poultry farm eggs," said Sunanda.

"Yeah, we have reared a pair of local fowls at home. You know, it's a must for fighting our protein deficiency," said Surabala.

The commercial break was over. The serial resumed. The fade-in on the screen was the prison of Kangsh. Bereaved and wailing Daibaki was slowly losing her senses. A helpless Vasudeva was sprinkling water on her eyes and massaging her head as a solace. The *Mahabharata* episode of the day ended there. But a lively discussion on the character, Kangsh, continued till Surendra and Sunanda rose to leave.

"Why must you leave right now? Let's have lunch together," Narendra said.

"No, not today. We'll be happy to have lunch with you, but let's plan it some other day. We have an appointment with the doctor today. Why don't you host a proper feast? We expect a big treat from you as your new home is ready," gushed Surendra. "Oh certainly. We'll host one on a holiday," Narendra said. "Wait a moment! We're early and will be kept waiting at the doctor's chamber. Why don't we have a quick look around the newly-built house? We too have a plan to build one," said Sunanda. "It's our pleasure to show you around."

Narendra and Surabala led the guests to the dining room, the kitchen, bedrooms and the in-house temple—one by one. The bamboo basket placed in front of the Radha-Krishna idol was full of freshly plucked flowers. Half-open fresh blossoms or full buds about to burst into bloom hung limp, almost resembling a string of little heads from beheaded babies—a *mundamala*![14] Was that a trickle of a teardrop glistening on the soft blossoms? Tears? All the flowers...all of them hung their lolling heads together.

*

Animatedly discussing the 'vastu' of the house, the four of them stepped on to the kitchen garden in the backyard. Narendra and Surabala briefed the guests with all finer details of the house. Surendra and Sunanda were glued to his words. The blueprint of a dream house seemed to take shape in a flash. Adjacent to the left corner of the boundary wall stood a small poultry shed. Its roof was put together with throwaway tin cans of mustard oil, embossed with the trade-mark, *Tripti*! The walls were of wire mesh. A pair of snow-white fowls was inside.

Not one or two, but a brigade of four approached them. The scared hen in captivity became frenetic. She moved from corner

---

14 Mundamala: A string of human heads which adorn the naked breast of Goddess Kali.

to corner fluffing out her feathers, shedding many of them. She poked the cock and warned it of the impending danger. Finding no way out, the mother hen went round the just-laid egg—once, twice, many times, in quick succession. At last, she covered the egg with her bosom and started incubating it. Like every other day, the cock continued to gaze out, its beak pushed out through an open grid in the mesh. He kept gazing at the fragment of sky resembling a frayed denim rag, peeping through the juncture of the two moss-covered walls. It gazed and waited, perhaps with the faint hope of an oracle and redemption.

THE REVERSE VEDA

Khyber Pass

*L*eading from the front was the snow-white horse for sacrifice, running at a great speed. It sped like an arrow whose umbilical cord had just got severed from the womb of a bow. Lashed by the strong wind, the mane of the galloping horse resembled thousands of arrows in reverse. Thunder boomed in the sky overhead with a deafening roar. With the spears in their hands poised to attack, the Aryan cavalry was closely following the horse. They had set off without any particular destination in mind through hazardous terrains and difficult mountain passes.

"Giddy-up!" The fastest rider galloping very close to the sacrificial horse was Indra, leader of the army. He had a spear strung from his shoulder. His aquiline nose was no less pointed than the razor-sharp copper blade of his spear. The maroon horse that Indra was riding was literally flying, and so were his unbound golden hair and beard—almost like a blazing inferno! The tanned tiger fur he was clad in flew like a flag, reeking of ferocity. Flying overhead in the sky was his most trusted messenger, Suvarna. True to the name, the winged spy looked like a golden beam of sunlight. The avian friend was a hawk – a bird of prey – whose special power of vision wouldn't allow even an ant to go unnoticed. Another trusted messenger of Indra was a bitch, Sarama. She ran alongside the right flank of Indra. Holding the bridle of the horse in one hand and the bones from

Dadhichi[15]'s torso shaped into a deadly weapon (Vajra) in the other, Indra thundered, "March forward...." As he shook the Vajra in the air, a gale began to blow in forceful gusts through the ribs of the weapon. The copper blades of the spears glittered in a flash of lightning followed by a deafening thunderbolt. A big tree burst into flames. An indifferent Indra didn't care to look back while a heavy downpour lashed the land.

Following Indra closely on his heels were his assistants— Agastya, Atreya, Kanva, Shandilya, Angiras, Madhu Chhanda, Gautam and other *rishis*. All were fierce nomadic fighters as well as composers of the sacred Vedic *riks* or hymns. Other Aryan warriors and women, including Indrani, were following them. The children were being carried on the backs of the adults. Two little puppies from Sarama's litter accompanied them. At the rear end of the cavalry were all the elders, including Indra's father. Their hearts throbbed fast.

The white horse stopped after crossing a mountain pass. Indra raised the Vajra as a command for all to stop. Suvarna circled a few extra rounds in the sky overheard before perching on Indra's shoulder—a safe site for him! The Aryans, birds of passage, erected make-shift camps by pegging tents made of animal fur. They set their horses free to graze on the lush green grass. The horse was an embodiment of the free spirit. While grazing along with other horses in the field, the youthful stallion was on the lookout for his mate for the night. The two suckling puppies of Sarama, on the other hand, began to suckle breathlessly while

---

15 Dadhichi: Sage Dadhichi or Dadhyancha is an important figure in Hindu mythology. He was one of the greatest devotees of Lord Shiva and offered his life in hard meditation to win the favours of Shiva who finally granted rishi Dadhichi his wish with His divine blessings. The bones of Dadhichi are a symbol of divine power. Lord Indra, the King of the Heavens, has the Vajra as his patent weapon, which is supposed to have been shaped out of the bones of Dadhichi. Indra's Vajra is the symbol used on India's highest military award for gallantry—the Param Vir Chakra.

their mother simply lay down on the ground and started licking her young puppies lovingly.

"What place is this?" Indra asked the rishis. "This is Khyber Pass," said Agastya. "This mountain pass has been named after the two Ashvins or Ashwini Kumars[16] of the Vedas," Agasthya added. Other elderly rishis too nodded their heads in agreement. The rishis, who could tame all natural forces with their special powers, then started chanting their self-composed verses to appease the Rain God in order to stop the downpour. Others followed suit. The rishis were famous for their sharp retentive memory; they could retain a hymn or mantra forever. Other Aryans, however, would have to rehearse mantras repeatedly to memorise them.

With the rain stopping after a while, the rishis bade good-bye to the setting sun with the Suryamantra hymn.[17] The Agnihotris ignited a *yajna*[18] for each Aryan lineage. The food habits of different Aryan *gotras*[19] weren't the same. The rishis chanted mantras appeasing Agnidev, the fire god, in the yajna pits of their respective gotras. After the Agni Puja, they started roasting the

---

16 Ashvins or Ashwini Kumars: They are two Vedic gods—twin divine horsemen of the Rigveda, born of the union of Vishwakarma's daughter Saranya (a goddess of the clouds) and Surya. They appear in golden chariots before sunrise and avert human misfortune and sickness. The Ashvins can be compared with the twins Castor and Pollux of classical Greco-Roman mythology. The divine twins Ašvieniai in Lithuanian mythology are direct counterparts of the Vedic Ashvins. Both names derive from the same Proto-Indo-European root for the horse—ek'w.

17 Suryamantra: Mantras to appease the Sun God.

18 Yajna: Special form of worship to appease the wrathful gods by building a large fire in a firepit and adding ghee, honey, rice and other ingredients to the fire, accompanied by the chanting of Vedic mantras and prayers. In the olden days a yajna would generally be preceded by an animal sacrifice. Yajnas are held during weddings, last rites and other such religious functions.

19 Gotra: Refers to kinship and a single Hindu lineage adhering to the patri-lineal form of descent; refers to a clan descending from an unbroken male line, usually starting with a sage like Agastya, Vishwamitra, Kashyap, Jamadagni, Vashishtha, etc. Originating from the concept of 'cow shelter' (called *gotra* in the *Rigveda*)—a large herd of people with one common ancestor. Earlier the *gotra* lineage was restricted only to the Brahmins, Kshatriyas (both warriors and administrators) and Vaishyas. Marrying within the same *gotra* is considered to be incest even in modern Hindu society as all are siblings.

flesh of animals from the day's catch, in their respective yajna fire pits. While calves were a forbidden stuff for Aryans belonging to Gautam gotra, ox meat was a taboo for the Shandilyas as was tiger meat for those belonging to Vyaghra gotra. The Aryans refrained from hunting the totemic animals of their respective gotras. The forefathers of these gotras were sacred. Beef, on the other hand, was forbidden food for each and every Aryan gotra.

They started eating the roasted meat. The women cooled the food before feeding their young ones. Alcohol and meat, as often as not, make a perfect match in contemporary society. This trend was no different among the Ayrans. They started to drink *somarasa*[20] to wash down the fire-roasted meat. Both men and women were drinking, singing and dancing around the yajna fires. Their tired children were fast asleep. Under the influence of the strong somarasa, Indra grew wilder. He started to shout and asked the rishis to sing hymns praising him. "What have you written about me?" Indra asked the rishis imperiously.

The rishis started chanting hymns to appease their leader. While a sage had christened Indra as the Rain God because he happened to step on to a new country amidst a heavy downpour, another named sage Dadhichi's bones as the Vajra (thunderbolt), because of its thundering effect.

Catching Indra sleeping, his old father dared to satiate his thirst for the somarasa of special fragrance, exclusively meant for the group leader. He started to pilfer the liquor of his son and drink. Indra, however, caught his father while stealing the somarasa. Indra went berserk, held his father by the legs and dragged him to the spot where he was stealing somarasa from. Scarlet with rage, Indra splashed somarasa on his father's mouth and shouted

---

20 *Somarasa*: The intoxicating juice of a creeper called soma.

at the top of his voice: "Drink as much as you can. Why hide and drink?" The poor father's body was totally drenched.

All of a sudden, an inebriated Indra threw away the empty pot of somarasa, took the sharpest spear propped against his seat and speared it through the chest of his father. The old man flopped to the ground like a deer pierced by an arrow, had his eyes set on his son and breathed his last. The wild dancing and singing came to an abrupt end. Indra wrenched the spear out of his father's chest. The blood from the lifeless body flowed into the rocky ground of Khyber Pass. The horrendous incident was enough to reduce the other elders in the Aryan force to a nervous wreck. A deathly silence filled the entire place. The dumbstruck rishis went to their respective tents. Indra noticed that the eyes of his father's body were still set on him. He sat near the body for a long while with a heavy heart and closed the eyes with his right palm.

The faithful horses, including the one meant for sacrifice, guarded the body through the night. While Suvarna was fast asleep perching on top of Indra's tent – its roost – with its beak hidden under the wings, Sarama lay across the door of Indra's tent with her two puppies.

Purandar

The rising sun dawned upon the land of the Saptasindhu – the area demarcated by the rivers Saraswati, Satadru, Bipasa, Asikani, Harappa, Bitasta and the Sindh – unfolding its beauty on this bright day. Riding their horses through the alluring green valley – a mosaic of rivers, green fields and woods – the Aryans were lost for words. They were surprised to see the sunlit valley teeming with life. The Indus Valley slowly tapered down the mountains and met the seven rivers. Fed by six youthful rivers in spate during the rainy season, the Sindh river charged ahead in full spleandour. The river frequently flooded its catchment areas and submerged some houses. The fields looked green with standing crops. On the bank of the river there were around a hundred villages surrounding the great cities of Mohenjo-Daro and Harappa.

"What a beautiful land! A world in itself, with a difference!" exclaimed Indra, astonished at the visual beauty. "Who would imagine such a beautiful world – a lush green valley completely shielded and protected by mountains and seas from all sides – lay for us to discover!"

The sacrificial horse began to canter down the hill, closely followed by the entire Aryan force. Indra was inspecting the neat and clean thatched mud houses in the villages. Young cowherds were busy shaping clay idols out of the fertile alluvial soil of the riverfed plains while their herds of cattle grazed in the fields. Both young and old were engaged in various activities—games, housework, meditaion, astrology, work in the fields...

"Who are the dwellers of this strange land?" Indra questioned the rishis.

"It's very difficult to identify them from afar," said some of the rishis. "Most of them have a dusky complexion and some seem to have a creamy-yellow skin tone."

"Oh that sounds rather strange! Surely they're non-Aryans. This beautiful land should be reserved only for the Aryans."

"Those selling their produce in the market are perhaps from Phoenicia—a country by the Mediterranean Sea. These merchants have sailed out to different parts of the world in boats carved out of cedar wood for trade and business. In the course of their journey they have reached this beautiful valley as well," explained the rishis to Indra.

"There seems to be a rich city! Oh, there's another, a bit farther away," pointed the rishis excitedly.

Noticing a new invading force galloping down from the north, the inhabitants of the Indus Valley went berserk. Amidst the sound of drums and conch shells sounding as alarms, people ran helter-skelter. Children playing in fields rushed back home while the older males scrambled up north with arms. With courage in the face of adversity, within moments, the villagers turned soldiers. They swooped down on the Aryans before the invading rishis could enter their villages. The Aryan rishis however, were skilled warriors and warmongers. They were overjoyed with the non-Aryans of the valley waging a war against them. They too retaliated with full vigour. Highly skilled in fencing, Indra's sword was rendered almost invisible, chopping off the heads and limbs of the Indus Valley non-Aryans. The killing spree of the Aryan rishis ran riot and the non-Aryans suffered a heavy casualty in the fierce battle.

The standing crops in the fields were destroyed and villagers who dared to confront the raging Aryans were killed, their houses torched in thousands and many of their women abused and raped. Many children lost their lives and the Aryans didn't spare even lactating mothers while the mayhem continued.

"These are demons," thundered Indra, supreme commander of the ethnic cleansing spree. About an hour before dusk, the Aryans reached the villages of the Kirats (hunters). Being traditional archers, the Kirats were a force to reckon with. They stood before the marauding Aryan army with bows and arrows, but how long could they last in front of Indra and his army in their own game? It took less than an hour for the Aryans to wipe them out! Those who survived fled to the east and the north.

The Aryans pegged their tents there and thus began their evening ritual of lighting fires, chanting their prayers while roasting meat and feasting on grilled meat and somarasa. For being able to destroy and torch hundred *puras* (villages) in a single day, the rishis christened Indra—Purandar. Melodious songs followed, to appease the great Purandar.

Britrohar

Next morning, the sacrificial horse started to run towards the south. For the Aryans the movement of the horse meant good luck, more human habitations with more wealth to loot; but not without waging a war. They followed the horse amidst thunder and lightning. The horse stood still in front of the main gate of Mohenjo-Daro. There were ramparts and trenches all around the city, and the only gate leading to the city had a lion's head on two sides. The brave Aryans marvelled at the technological excellence in the peripheral security setup of the city.

Suddenly big stones started raining down on them from the other side of the trenches and they were forced to step back. It was instantly followed by an attack from skilled archers, who literally showered sharp arrows on the invaders from strategic battlements. The Aryans too retaliated in a befitting way but failed to make much headway in the counterattack, as they had to fight without seeing their opponents positioned at strategic locations. Before it was too late, Indra and his men came to understand that victory would elude them if they didn't enter the city. But how? This question continued to haunt Indra. Who could afford to lose a visible treasure? Going back with the Horse meant lowering the dignity of the Aryans, and opting to a life full of misery. Defeat for Indra? A bitter pill for him to swallow! Indra looked at his men who too had their eyes set on him. An astute war strategist, Indra looked around and saw a big embankment that looked like a gigantic serpent. The embankment protected the city from the wrath of the Sindh that roared fiercely down, sounding almost like a captive lion. Indra found an ace up his sleeve. A dirty trick!

He drank as much *somarasa* as he could, took a spear, climbed on top of the embankment and then jumped into the river amidst the rolling waves. He began to hit the base of the embankment with his spear very hard. There was not much headway as the turbulent water constantly pushed him out. A tenacious Indra continued to strike the embankment with the spear. Other Aryan saboteurs pitched in as well. At last they were able to bore a big hole in the base of the embankment. Standing on top of the embankment, Indra shook the skeleton of Dadhichi's torso followed by deafening thunder and a brilliant flash of lightning in the sky. Moments later, the embankment collapsed and Indra fell when the land beneath his feet gave way. He fractured one of his jaws in the accident. The injury was, however, not severe enough to hold him back. The surging waters of the Sindh ran amok like a huge herd of cattle, breaking open the main gate of Mohenjo-Daro with the first rush of waves. Victorious in his devious design, Indra literally rode into the city on the waves of the manmade flash flood. Other rishis followed suit and a fierce battle began. In face-to-face wars, no warriors could stand long in front of the Aryans. The dwellers of the city were victims of twin attacks—attacks from the Aryans as well as the devastating deluge caused by the rushing river. With the unarmed city dwellers fleeing to safer areas, the Aryans began to blindly slay the ethnic dark-skinned people of the valley—the Kirats and the Ponis. They continued to behead the non-Aryans, not even sparing the women and children. Experienced practitioners of killing and looting, the mayhem and arson in the ethnic cleansing failed to make any humane appeal to the Aryan conscience.

The city – full of life with flourishing trade and business till a few moments ago – now wore a deserted look. Those aware of secret escape routes left for Harappa. The Aryan warriors then turned plunderers and looters. While looting the houses of the Ponis, they got seals with inscription of alphabets on them. They started to examine and study the alphabets with rapt attention. The Aryans were particularly overjoyed at discovering thousands of cows from the cattle sheds of the Ponis and began to dance in the water, slapping each others' backs to celebrate their victory.

Since Indra emerged as the unrivalled winner by breaching the embankment (*britro*), Rishi Madhuchhanda named him Britrohar. The rishi scripted a *rik* with the new name and started to sing that.

Rishi Shandilya, on the other hand, named him Apasujit, since he conquered the new city riding on the surging waters of the Sindh. He too scripted a rik with the name, and sang the paean. The waters soon spread across the fields, but ebbed with the receding pull of the flood, laying bare roads and fields rendered more fertile than ever with the residual soil of the flooding river. The rich green fields and hills made the sacrificial horse unwilling to move. The Aryans too found no reason to leave fertile Sindh. They settled down comfortably in the well-built empty houses and bid their nomadic life adieu.

Ahalya

Like every other day, Rishi Gautam left for the riverside to say his morning prayers in the wee hours. His bulky body soon blended with the darkness. His wife Ahalya, on the other hand, was still in bed, savouring the last few moments of early morning slumber. Well aware that Rishi Gautam would take not less than an hour to return, she stringed together a garland of sweet dreams for herself. Gradually the staccato *tapa-tap* of a galloping horse's hooves from a distance merged with the remnants of her fading dream and came to a halt in the courtyard.

Rat-a-tat-tat...the door opened with a screeching sound. The untimely opening of the door brought Ahalya back to her senses. "Why so early!? What happened to the rishi today?" she asked herself.

Moments later a shocked Ahalya sat on the bed, looking right into the eyes of the Aryan leader, Indra! This was what she had been apprehensive of all along. Her broken dreams lay scattered in pieces on the bed. All her efforts at escaping proved futile. Indra was agile enough to block all her escape routes. Finally, skilled warrior that she was, Ahalya attacked Indra like a cornered cat. However, with the leader of the Aryans as her opponent she was like a clay doll. She locked her hands with Indra in a scuffle, but her tender fingers got twisted in the iron grip of the mighty male. Ahalya's brassiere loosened and beneath his long golden locks, Indra's lustful eyes blazed like flicks of fire at her bared body. Ahalya was familiar with the lustful instinct of Aryan males. Her face, bare breasts and thighs burnt under the scorching glare of Indra. Within a few moments, a male python started coiling around her body and hot, passionate gusts of breath blew across her face, breasts, belly-button...

When all her efforts to shake off the rapist failed, Ahalya began screaming at the top of her voice till she fell unconscious. Thus her limp senseless body lay listlessly, inviting Indra to explore and ravage it at his will. With his loyal horse standing guard in the courtyard and the trusted Suvarna keeping vigil by perching on a tree outside, Indra satiated his lust.

*

Meanwhile, the high-pitched screams of Ahalya had made Gautam rush home. What had gone amiss with his beloved Ahalya!? As his bulky body raced home, gaining momentum every moment, an alert Suvarna started flapping his wings. The horse too became restless and started pawing the ground impatiently. Upon his arrival, Gautam spotted Indra leaving the house with a sly smile playing around his lips. Enraged, the sage read the smile right and knew that the Aryan leader had had his lust fully satiated. He attacked Indra with all his might. The group leader, on the other hand, simply made a quick escape by riding away on his horse. Suvarna accompanied him, flying overhead. After a hot chase, an angry Gautam pointed his index finger at Indra and spat fire. He cursed him, pronouncing that he would lose his male genitals and instead be covered all over with foul-smelling female genital organs. Indra just laughed aloud. Like every other day, his pre-dawn mating adventure was enveloped in the dark.

Alighting from the horse, Indra saw a fuming Indrani standing at the door, blocking the entrance. Her ageing, sagging breasts heaved with rage and passion. The dimly-lit dawn could seal Indra's sexual adventure from all, but Indrani. He stood erect for a while. As he strided in, Indrani blocked the door with her arms stretched across it. An indifferent Indra made his way into the house by removing her hand with complete disregard for her dignity and sentiments. Furious at Indra's behaviour, Indrani bit one of Indra's hands and scratched his chest with her sharp nails like a wild cat. Indra simply laughed at her and entered the house. Indrani remained steadfast and said, "Oh lord, you have blessed women with sharp nails and teeth, but what made you stop short of adding poison to them?"

She went out to the courtyard; her home was no longer a peaceful refuge for her, it was a prison. She might be Indrani to others but was no more than a rag to Indra. At a tender age, she had seen two other senior Indras, who too were brutal but they hadn't been totally devoid of conscience like the present one. She spotted Suvarna perched atop their house, preening himself.

She picked up a stone in her rage and threw it at Indra's avian friend. Suvarna just leaned sideways and avoided the salvo. After a while, Indra's waiting horse caught her notice and she began beating the poor animal black and blue with the broken branch of a tree.

Unable to trace the 'promiscuous' woman's identity Indrani left the house in the dark to look for her. The faithful Sarama with her two puppies came forward on her own to lead her lady along.

The author of melodious hymns, sage Gautam, on the other hand, went berserk. Unable to trace Indra he turned back homewards and began looking for Ahalya, who had, however, left home. Her upper garment lay in the ruthlessly crumpled bed. The rishi searched each and every corner of the house, but to no avail. The rear door of the house banged in the gusts of wind. Gautam went out and called out her name... "Ahalya, Ahalya". The sound reverberated in the folds of the Sindh Valley and hit the hills, but there was no response. In his whirlwind search for his wife, Gautam scanned almost all bushes, scrubs and hill troughs nearby. Ahalya was nowhere to be seen.

The rising sun slowly wiped the thin darkness away. "Hide, if you can," Gautam challenged his wife by gnashing his teeth. He caught a whiff of the familiar *chengi*[21] of Ahalya as he crossed the hill. Following the smell of the chengi he set his feet on the two cliffheads between which Ahalya was hiding. Reduced to a nervous wreck, she managed to whisper with folded hands, "I did nothing, my lord. I'm innocent."

Gautam brushed aside all pleas of Ahalya. "You haven't done anything! You're a concubine of Indra," the rishi shouted, attempting to drag her out of the narrow ledge but failing to

---

21 *Chengi*: A traditional hair conditioner prepared with water used for washing uncooked rice and certain herbs with a sweet fragrance.

do so. The passage was too small to allow his bulky body to pass through. Standing on the rocks, he began to stone Ahalya, his beloved wife. The sharp stones turned the tender and bare body of the woman into a mangled mass of blood and bones. Accumulating all the strength she was left with, Ahalya told the Sun god with hands folded: "My lord, you're omniscient. I've no complaint of dying, but I leave you with the responsiblity to spread the word that I'm innocent."

"Innocent! Innocent! Humm..." roared Gautam. Ahalya's wails and screams, however, went unheard. She was buried alive under a heap of stones.

At that moment Indrani rushed to the spot, following Sarama. "Ahalya! No! She could never be promiscuous." She made an attempt to prevent Gautam from killing her. Sage Gautam literally threw Indrani away and picking up another stone, threw it at Ahalya. Left with no alternative, Indrani took a big rock and hit Gautam from behind to settle the score against adulterous Indra. Gautam fell unconscious on the heap of stones. Indrani swooped down to rescue Ahalya from her stone-grave but to no avail.

A blind and limping sun rose slowly overhead in Aryavarta, sealing the fate of two women.

Haruyipia

Haruyipia or Harappa was no less developed than Mohenjo-Daro in wisdom, science and technology. The city stood on the bank of the river Harappa, known in different places with different names—Paresni, Rasa and Harappa or Haruyipia. Harappa had more Phoenicians than Mohenjo-Daro. They did a roaring business in dairy products. Rishi Madhuchhanda informed Indra of the livestock found aplenty in Harappa. The greed for livestock made Indra, who was deeply engrossed in satiating his carnal lust under the drunken influence of somarasa, restless. The vast grasslands of Sindh, on the other hand, made the sacrificial horse lethargic and unwilling to move on. It wasn't ready to run for fresh adventures. With continued provocation from other rishis, Indra was in a haste to go and conquer Harappa. Weighing all options one morning, he sent Suvarna to Harappa. Harappa was a small flight away from Mohenjo-Daro for Suvarna. Flapping its golden wings, the hawk made a sortie.

However, on that day, the avian messenger kept the Aryans waiting till afternoon. A restless and tired Indra and other rishis had their eyes set on the sky. The rishis discussed the delay in the arrival of Suvarna, adding their own explanations to the episode.

Shading his eyes with his palm, Indra finally spotted the wings of Suvarna high up in the sky. He heaved a sigh of relief, so did other rishis. Like every other day, Suvarna took some extra rounds and perched on the forearm of Indra. All the rishis, including Indra, leaned expectantly towards the hawk. Suvarna however, did not convey any message to his master. Indra could accurately decipher each and every gesture, hooting and flapping of wings of the bird. But on that day, the mysterious behaviour of the mute bird made him look on helplessly. Finally losing his patience, Indra had a close look at the bird to find that it was dozing—a most unexpected behaviour on its part. Enraged, Indra got hold of the bird by its legs, struck it against the ground and kicked it. The bird fell on the ground like a dead mass, ejected the food – a lump of paneer or cottage cheese – it had had in Harappa, took a lingering look at his master and fell unconscious. Indra made no mistake in guessing that the cunning Phoenicians had rendered Suvarna dumb by feeding it paneer.

*

The very next day, Indra sent Sarama to Harappa. The news of the arrival of a snow-white bitch at the main gate of Harappa spread like wildfire in the city. Haruyipians had never seen such a beautiful white dog with thick, long hair. The door of the city opened and Sarama entered. The armymen manning the gate and others in the city made an effort to catch her. Skilled in hypnotism, Sarama knew how to woo people. She started frisking and playing hide-and-seek on the roads with the animal lovers of the civilised city. In her playful activities, she didn't fail to take stock of the big cattle sheds and dairy farms in the city. Within a short period, she became the darling of the masses and started to hop from the lap of one woman to that of another. There was no bar for Sarama in the city. She could even enter one's kitchen without any hesitation. Chained by the affection of the womenfolk, Sarama got rid of the shackles of the army. Delicious dishes were offered to woo her. She cleverly tried to impress upon the minds of the Haruyipians that she would never desert them. However, taking stock of the fortunes of Haruyipia, she successfully bluffed her way through, and quietly left for Mohenjo-Daro. The thought of her puppies haunted her at the back of her mind.

This time it wasn't the sacrificial horse but Sarama who led the Aryan warriors to Haruyipia at midnight. When they reached Haruyipia, Indra saw that the security arrangements of the city were no different from that of Mohenjo-Daro. The city was well protected with high trenches and forts, and the main gate was strong enough to foil misadventure of any sort. Indra asked the Aryan warriors to hide behind big trees. He hinted at Sarama to go to the main gate of the city with her two puppies. Sarama followed the diktat and started to bark in front of the gate. Finding Sarama back, that too, with two cute and frisky puppies scampering behind her, the guards manning the gate were overjoyed. They opened the gate and allowed her to enter. As soon as Sarama entered the city with her puppies, Indra and the other Aryan warriors rushed in before the guards could close the heavy gate. Moments later, Harappa turned into an open slaughter house where the skilled Aryan warriors were on the rampage, chopping thousands of innocent non-Aryans, including women and children, into pieces. Besides killing innocent people, they took away cattle and other livestock of the city. The brute Aryan force set afire the cattle sheds and houses. The non-Aryans and the Phoenicians had no alternative but to flee. The Aryans continued to chase and kill them. Egged on by a wind, the blazing inferno danced and crackled its destructive way down the alleys.

The non-Aryans were caught between the devil and the deep blue sea. If they could escape the inferno, the Aryans waited for them with swords and choppers. Indra quietly witnessed the burning of a thousand-year-old civilisation and the wave of misery it sparked off all around.

The city mayor, his staff and the elite Phoenicians who knew secret escape routes fled through them. Smelling a rat, the Aryans chased them. After a hot chase down one of these secret routes, Indra killed a Phoenician called Daos and took his daughter, Usha, with him. The Aryans, including Indra himself, were simply awestruck by Usha's extraordinary beauty. They had never seen such a beautiful girl among the Aryans. She was their prize catch of the day and the men crowded around her to have a closer look at her face and body.

Indra rode his horse again, held Usha tightly with his beefy left hand in front of him and resumed his chase of the fleeing Phoenicians and Harappans.

"Don't let the heathens flee...kill them. Cleanse this city. No child born of the heathen womb should be left alive on this land of the Aryans," Indra commanded his fellow soldiers.

Some ethnic people left for the southern hills while the seafaring Phoenicians opted to return to their western homeland across the seas, taking the riverine route through the Rasa and the Sindh with boats. They moved towards the Runn of Kutch. The Aryan riders chased them out of the river bank but had to stop as they were not skilled in the art of naval warfare.

Held tightly in Indra's left hand, Usha watched her fellow Phoenicians fleeing, leaving her behind. She cried her heart out. She was unaware of the fate that was to befall her.

Ashvamedha Yajna

With the passage of time, Aryavarta turned into a land of milk and honey. The Aryans arranged an Ashvameda Yajna (Sacrifice of Horse) at the year-end, an event hitherto unknown in this part of the world.

The wild, nomadic Aryans turned into permanent settlers in Aryavarta, their new-found land. Hordes of Aryan men and women turned up at the site of the yajna early in the morning, wearing beautiful clothes and jewellery. Pre-yajna activities – site sanctification and *bhoomipuja*[22] – took up the entire morning. The yajna began when the sun descended into the horizon, with the chanting of mantras by the priests, instantly pulling the crowd to the *yajnasthal*[23]. Sarama, on the other hand, lay down keeping a safe distance from the site and suckled her puppies. Seated on *kushasans*[24], Indra and Indrani threw their offerings into the sacrificial fire with the chant of the eternal mantra: "*Ohm swaha, ohm swaha, ohm swaha...*"

---

22 *Bhoomipuja*: Worshipping and sanctifying the land.

23 *Yajnasthal*: Spot of the *yajna* or sacrifice.

24 *Kushasan*: Floor mats woven out of dried reeds.

Sacrifices followed amidst the chanting of mantras. A rishi snatched one of the two puppies from Sarama, chopped it into two pieces and flung it into the fire, while a stunned Sarama watched helplessly. The Aryans broke the trust of the loyal and faithful Sarama who ran around, barking madly at the congregation. The other puppy too followed its mother with its tail between its legs. Sarama's wails failed to draw the attention of the mantra-chanting rishis; on no account could the yajna be stopped and anybody trying to create an impediment during the yajna would meet with a cruel death. Usha however, appalled at the brutality of the Aryans, made a quick getaway from the yajna site. Indrani, on the other hand, stayed put beside Indra like a statue.

The yajna continued. The rishis started to sacrifice goats, jackals and other beasts. The site of the yajna was stained red with sacrificial blood. At the end, the youthful snow-white sacrifial horse was brought in. The stallion looked around and trembling at the sight of blood, made an abortive attempt to flee and was immediately caught and held back. The partially revealed head of the stallion, circled by its wavy mane looked enchanting. Indra stained his thumb with the blood from the sacrificial post and marked it on the forehead of the horse. A copper plate full of wheat was served to the horse while the Aryans – with their eyes set on the horse – chanted *ashvastuti*[25]. They shouted "*Sadhu, sadhu*[26]" in excitement, as the confused horse finally started eating out of the copper plate. "*Ohm swaha, ohm swaha, ohm swaha...*"

An elated Indra and the other rishis drowned themselves in somarasa and continued to chant mantras. Indrani and the other assembled women bathed the horse with clean water, sponged

---

25 *Ashvastuti*: Verses appeasing horse.
26 *Sadhu, sadhu*: Well done.

it with the edges of their clothes, massaged its body with ghee and decorated it with garlands and ornaments. Finally, Indrani was back in her seat. Amidst the chanting of mantras, the priest inched towards the horse and dragged it to the sacrificial post. The bloodstained chopper in the hands of the priest made the horse uneasy and it made a last attempt to flee. The rishis caught it by the legs and held it in the trap. Amid the chanting of mantras, the blowing of conch shells and the jingle of bells, the chopper fell on the neck of the horse. Blood gushed out like the waters of the Sindh, Shatadru and the Bipasa and flowed into the soil. An inebriated Indra shouted with joy and the other rishis followed suit. The rishis then made scars all around the carcass that was deftly cut into pieces. The hour of Agnihotri had come. The flesh of the horse and other animals were burnt and offered as *prasad*[27].

An ashvastuti followed... "Oh God, let this new-found land be fertile with the blood of the sacrificial holy horse and be transformed into a land of milk and honey, full of ripe golden corn. Let our stables be full of strong horses. Let the semen of the horse give birth to Aryans as strong as stallions."

As all the Aryans enjoyed the burnt meat, a stunned sacrificial horse – the designate for the year ahead – remained a mute witness to the entire process of the yajna. Trembling with an unknown fear, the stallion quietly sped off at breakneck speed to the east.

---

27 *Prasad*: Holy food sanctified by divine blessings.

FISH OF A DEAD RIVER

*S*unday morning. Rolling out of bed, Rajen glanced at the wall clock. It was 9:40 a.m. He massaged his head with both palms put together, finding no trace of hair, even with his palms travelling a good way up his head, which lay like a barren stretch of land. His life was an odyssey from the position of a clerk to the superintendent, a slow and steady grind—never in a hurry to overtake his seniors. It was natural that ageing would cast a shadow on him.

Seema placed a cup of lemon tea on the table. Taking small sips, Rajen strode out to the verandah, limp and heavy-footed. He lit a cigarette and flopped down in the armchair. The fat deposits in his bloated body shook, like a tremor rocking the earth's surface. He stretched and yawned, his breath still reeking of strong alcohol—typical of the defence stores. He had resorted to binge drinking the night before. In the past, to dodge Seema, he had had to chew on fennel seeds – *saunf* – to hide the sharp reek of a couple of strong pegs. As he hit the bottle, the empty liquor bottles lined up erect like sleepless sentinels in his bedroom through the night. Seema had been forced to issue him the NOC long back.

Taking a long drag at his cigarette, Rajen stared at the lake. The sunshine outside was scorching. The shimmering blue water of the lake dazzled like the silver veil of a night club dancer. The water looked clean and distilled, but the bottom of the lake was full of thick algae. This hard fact would always deceive the one who had never dared to swim in the lake.

Offices, residential quarters and small shops selling grocery and other daily necessities sprang up in rows, on either side of the lake. Till the recent past, this was a sleepy hamlet still clinging on to the last vestiges of its past glory. Angling in the lake, sitting under a giant kapok tree, was a brawny giant of a man. A vulture perched on one of the upper branches of the tree he was sitting under. The fishing rod and the bobber floated, holding the bait at the right depth. The bait, made of waste extracted from brewing country liquor, was unfailing. Rajen noticed the angler daily, morning and evening, sitting quietly at the same spot. He often caught big fish. A young man now sat next to him, asking questions. Puffing on his cigarette, Rajen listened to snippets of the conversation between the two with rapt attention.

"The water looks quite calm, without the bubbles and ripples raised by moving fish. Would you be able to hook any fish in such quiet waters?" the youth asked the angler.

"Certainly. But of course, the big ones go down much deeper and stay there. Algae has grown so thick that if a man happens to fall in, one should give him up for good. Fish can hardly swim across the green blanket and come to the surface. When there was a current..." the angler broke off halfway.

"Current?" the youth blurted out in astonishment.

"Yes. This wasn't a dead river. The river Rukmini followed its own arched course. When both ends of the stream got constricted, some government labourers, accompanied by some local miscreants, closed the mouth and let the river go straight. That made the river dry up and a sulking Ganga deserted us for ever!" the man explained.

"Oh, I see. It wasn't a case of the remote past!" the youth said in a bemused voice.

"No, no. Not even forty years! When there was a strong current, silver fish could be spotted playing and swimming in shoals regularly. There was no trace of algae," the man replied.

"It can be freed from algae even now," the young man suggested lightly.

"Making it free of algae?" the angler stared at him in astonishment. "Yes, it should perhaps be done. You, the young brigade, should hitch up your pants and come forward with spades. Let the Rukmini follow its own natural course without hiderance," he added.

"Right." Rajen tapped the butt end of the cigarette on the ashtray and immersed himself in his thoughts.... "The youth should come forward!" This was an oft-repeated phrase for the dashing student leader Rajen, some twenty-five years ago during his heady days of youth. Rajen marvelled at the angler being no less of a philosopher. Clear all algae in canals, ponds, lakes, rivers and in homes. Clear the one that hangs like dirty cottonwool under my eyebrows and clear my vision....

Smitten suddenly by the prick of conscience, Rajen's distraught mind cried out.

He instinctively pressed the cigarette hard against the ashtray. "Why don't you brush your teeth! It's 10 o'clock," Seema appeared in the verandah and chided him busily.

"Umm..." Rajen responded listlessly, not moving from his armchair.

"It's a holiday. Why don't you help the boy with his lessons?" Seema demanded to know after a while.

"Why should I? Don't the tutors teach him?"

"Theirs is routine teaching. The kid is fond of your teaching."

"Fond of my teaching?" Rajen sat upright and took notice of Piku, his ten-year-old son. He was waiting near the door with a book. His blue eyes beamed with hope. Piku was a meritorious lad gifted with a rare yearning for knowledge. He would go a long way, if properly guided. However, Piku was denied any sort of paternal guidance. In fact, Rajen avoided his son to an extent, always apprehensive of his bad habits getting transmitted to his son. Seema, however, felt that Rajen no longer loved his son. She was under the impression that people who were much too fond of drinking and labelled as 'boozers' were bereft of any affection for their children. With a smile Rajen called his son, who wasted no time to come and sit on his father's lap.

"Which sum do you want explained and to work at?" Rajen asked his son only to be taken aback and left bemused when Piku replied, "Moral science, not mathematics."

"You mean moral study! Hmm..." Rajen stared at Seema, his eyes wide till Piku's hair bristled against his chin. He came back to his senses and passed the buck to Seema. "Piku, go to your mom. She will explain the lesson to you."

"No no, I can't," Seema rejected outright.

"Why not? You had 'education' as a subject for your Bachelor's degree. That apart, you had a brief stint as a teacher in a private school before joining the government job. Even if you have forgotten..." Rajen couldn't complete his sentence as a sullen Seema glared at him.

"Hmm...it's okay. Piku, I will engage another tutor from tomorrow for moral studies and literature. Put your book away now," Rajen stammered. The poor boy went back into the house sullenly. No sooner had Piku left the place than Rajen raised his voice against Seema.

"Have you gone crazy?" he barked at her. "How can I teach my son moral studies? Why do you put me to shame before my own son?"

"Why can't you do that? What's lost if you just read and tell him the meaning?"

Seema's words were enough to make Rajen fire back. "Why can't...you do that? You too are a graduate!"

"Let's stop."

"What do you think? Is any morality left in this venal and drunkard father? For the past twenty-five years, I've not handled any file without a bribe. I utter hundreds of lies in the office. How can I advise my son not to tell a lie and teach him to stay away from doing anything illegal? Mahatma Gandhi, Vivekananda... huh..." Rajen seethed in angry frustration.

"Okay, no screaming!" Seema cut him short. "You could have just explained to him the text in the book!" she retorted brusquely.

"I could have done it, had it been twenty-five years ago. One can tell thousands of lies to others, but never to oneself." A one-time honest and idealistic student leader, Rajen was a frustrated father today. "Won't I be shamed," he continued, "when Piku follows my 'moral advice', accepting it verbatim in good faith? I do respect my son and don't wish to hoodwink him!"

"Well, I too, agree on that!" Seema replied.

"Don't ask me ever to teach Piku," Rajen pleaded. "If need be, I will engage more tutors—expense is no issue," he added, and limped towards the bathroom.

*

Rajen soon took a trip down memory lane in the solitude of the bathroom. Solitude rakes up memories. Brushing his teeth in front of the mirror, he recollected his life's rich pageant. "What an enviable persona it was!" The mask he put on was the root cause of all the troubles in his life. Nostalgia gripped him—a child Rajen gleaning dried 'cow-dung' cakes on the river bank, attending primary school with a slate pressed against the armpit, munching water lily and enjoying the affection of all for being an intelligent boy. His college life too flashed a quick appearance in his mind—the students' union, the language movement, court arrests, detention in examination, his first encounter with Seema, wild love, both graduating together and tying the knot in haste. Till their marriage they did follow an ideology.

Rajen married Seema while he was still without a job to support a family. While on the hunt for jobs and a steady income, he stepped into corruption raj, and then let all his reins loose. He managed to land a job by paying ten thousand rupees, which he had procured by selling three *bigha*s of arable land. Since then, he had been making quick bucks.

Soon after he was blessed with children. His old run-down family home was replaced with a new concrete structure and the area of his total arable land increased manifold. Television sets, fridges, cars, lucrative career promotions and a stable government job for Seema—all rushing in at the same time at the cost of peace in his family life. It was like an exercise geared at publicity—to let people know that Rajen and Seema could mint money by cleverly dodging income tax. Gradually the ailments of the rich and the aristocrats became a part of their lives. While Seema was struck by melena, Rajen suffered frequent heart attacks. They were blessed with children but never a cause of pride for them.

According to Rajen, children these days were ashamed of their parental identity. They shied away from letting others know about their parents. His eldest son was a brilliant boy, but had gone astray. He had become a prey to drinks, drugs and ganja and was considered to be a parasite to the family as well as to society. He didn't care about his father. Caught in flagrante, the daughter, on the other hand, made her father hang his head in shame. He had no choice but to leave her in his ancestral house; where stories about her sordid past did the rounds of the neighbourhood. Large financial contributions to the powerful social organisations in the area – the Mahasabha and the Sahityasabha – did, however, have an effect on the commoners who didn't dare to raise their voice against the 'scandal' openly. In an effort to plug all such holes in his life, Rajen was ready to go bankrupt, simply to ensure a smooth future for the rest of his children. He had to maintain his 'spotless' reputation in society – even though the effort burnt a large hole in his pocket – especially as a safeguard against the socially sensitive issue of the marriage of his children, which had to be arranged without disturbing social parameters and the weddings carried off smoothly.

This apart, he was in need of a strong platform as his foothold after retirement. His service days were numbered. His youngest son, Piku, was as precociously gifted and promised to be a brilliant student as the eldest son.... If he too went astray! Rajen's last hope! How utterly unfortunate would that be! Parents couldn't discipline their wards. They were apprehensive of their wards firing salvos at them! The entire generation was morally bankrupt. Wasn't there any way out of this gutter? Wasn't there anybody to uproot the filth and discard it for good? All were corrupt; society itself was corrupt to the core, with no fresh air to breathe. This suffocation, this was life!...

Breathing in deep, heavy gasps, Rajen returned from the bathroom and sat near the dining table, sipping his tea. Less sugar? Maybe it was just the bitterness in his mind!

"Where's Piku?" Rajen asked Seema.

"He was sitting in a huff in a corner of the verandah. Piku, Piku, where have you gone?"

Seema went out calling her son.

"Has he gone to the lakes? If he slips...! Can't you even keep an eye on...?" Rajen pushed the cup aside and went out looking for the boy.

"Mom, Dad...quick, come and see!" an excited voice rang out, calming down the anxious couple.

"Hurry up!" Piku shouted. Seema reached Piku first, followed by the bulky Rajen, gasping in his breathlessness.

"Look, a big fish swam out from behind a rock at the bottom of the lake. Wow! *Yaah* big!" An excited Piku clapped in joy.

"Oh, is that so?" Rajen and Seema, both quite stunned, exclaimed together. The fish first swam to the surface of the lake. It then shook its tail fin to get rid of the patches of algae clinging to it.

"It has come out! How did it manage to swim across such a thick blanket of algae? *Wah, wah!*" Rajen bubbled with enthusiasm and excitement.

The brawny angler came running and dangled his unfailing bait, almost straight at the mouth of the huge carp. The fish ignored it and kept playing in the silvery water, swimming with its ventral side up. Tumbling over in the joy of being freed of the stubborn blanket of algae, the fish suddenly glided past like a jet, leaving a trail of foamy current behind it in the dead river, momentary though!

"Lovely!" Rajen exclaimed, looking at the faint trail of current. He called out to his son, "Piku, dear, come on. What lesson would you like me to teach you? Let's go back and begin right now!"

DEATH OF CARPENTER DHVAJA

$\mathcal{T}$he wee hours of morning. The village slept soundly in the light haze of dewy darkness. The morning star twinkled against a dim eastern sky. All was silent, quiet, with not even a wisp of the gentle early morning breeze from the south. Leaning slightly forward on a staff in his right hand, octogenarian carpenter Dhvaja stood all alone, staring at his home. The loose end of his *khuttei*[28] and the hemlines of the shawl were motionless, so was the knot of the *nukun*[29]. His hair, eyebrows, moustache and beard were hoary white. The cataract in his eyes was, however, at its initial stage. Gifted with an ageless vision, he could see the house and the nails that he had hammered in, distinctly. His home was where his soul resided. He built his home with his hard-earned money with his own hands on his own land. It was the home where his dream to live longer was born and nourished. His home – his binoculars – were a window to his remote past. He glanced for the last time at his own creation. Perhaps this was why he was in a haste to savour a glance at each and every remarkable event of his past.

Having lost all – parents, kith and kin, and even the piece of land to build a dwelling – thirteen-year-old Dhvaja was a

---

28 *Khuttei*: A Bishnupriya Manipuri males' lower garment.
29 *Nukun* : A sacred thread worn across the body by Hindus.

vagabond. Working as a servant in the homes of Brojochan and Ballavgiri, the downy-cheeked boy grew into a strong, masculine youth. The independent mind of an able-bodied youth didn't allow him to continue with the life of a menial, a domestic servant.

At a *mahendrayoga*[30] on a Thursday, Dhvaja bowed down to Thabal – the master craftsman and carpenter of the village – for his bleassings, accepting him as his Guru. In a simple but solemn ceremony, he offered his craft-guru a cluster of bananas, a *khuttei* and a 25-paise coin.

Guru Thabal gave him a tearful send-off after a rigorous nine-year training. During the gurukul stint, the preceptor taught him everything of carpentry – right from the art of sharpening the chisel to the secret behind the magic touches – which lent buildings and cottages their desired look.

A year elapsed amidst hard work. Dhvaja purchased a half-bigha plot of land, erected a thatched house there and settled down permanently under his own roof. He added a bigha of arable land to his property. And with his rucksack loaded with tools, he went his own way, basking in the warmth of his high morale and boosted spirits.

Dhvaja built the house of Gambhir Singh of Tuk. Sabi, Gambhir Singh's daughter cooked and fed him the much-sought-after tasty curry of black lentils punched with a perfect Manipuri flavour, offering him spice-flavoured, tangy rolls of juicy betel-leaves blended with betel nuts to cleanse his mouth with, after the meal. Overcome by gratitude and much else, Dhvaja put his mind and soul to work. However, there were other attarctions too. One fine spring morning, Sabi's young waxen cheeks tinged with the colours of Holi caught his attention while the girl served Dhvaja

---

30 *Mahendrayoga*: An auspicious moment.

his humble meal of rice and curry. His eyes remained glued on her, expressing an unquenchable thirst for reciprocation.

Dhvaja worked on wooden planks, smoothening the pieces by shaving very thin slices off it. His strong and bare back, arms and shoulders would be drenched in sweat—the rippling, dancing muscles showing through the dark moist skin. Sabi would stand spellbound with a spicy betel-roll for Dhavja who turned back when he felt the warmth of Sabi's breath on his back. And their subtle courtship would begin in full swing. With a loving smile playing upon his lips, he would take the specially-spiced betel-roll from Sabi's shaking hand and start chewing it. His eyes would shut with the heady blend of areca nut, betel leaves and tobacco melting his senses; his ruddy-tinted lips would munch on, savouring the intoxicating flavour of betel leaves punched with the first flush of romance.

A bunch of sweet memories crowd in...

Dhvaja tying the main horizontal bar of the roof with a post. With a long strip of cane rolled in his left hand and his legs balanced against two erect poles, he pulls hard at the strip of cane with his teeth clenched. The sharp crackle of the cane strip embodies his perfect craftsmanship. Gambhir Singh is satisfied with the muscle power and craftmanship of the youth. "I may rest assured that the youth is strong enough to work hard and feed Sabi," he tells himself and makes no further delay in handing over his daughter to Dhvaja. Their wedding bells ring.

A beautiful newly-wedded bride and a reed-thatched house didn't make a good match, Dhvaja thought. To translate his dream house with wooden frames into a reality, Dhvaja started saving every penny. He handed over the day's earning to Sabi's cautious hands and the new bride set aside a little portion of that. She added to the savings by weaving garments and reaping paddy. Living an austere life and running her household with iron hands, she saved their hard-earned money in a pitcher kept underground.

Memories in flashback lead him on and he slips into a daydream.... Dhvaja thatches the roof of his house and Sabi lobs bunches of weeds to him.

"How many bunches are left?" Dhvaja asks Sabi.

"Only twenty-seven to go."

"Lob a few more."

Secured tight in the bunches of weeds, rolls of betel nut go up to Dhvaja from Sabi.

...The house-warming ceremony is on. After shifting to the new house, Dhvaja and Sabi feed some devotees. An elated Guru Thabal showers blessings on his disciple, Dhvaja. "My boy," he says. "I'm overwhelmed. The design speaks of a unique craftsmanship. I wish you a happy and long life in this house."

...Neighbours keep visiting in hordes just to see the design of the house. Playing hosts to the visitors, they have to buy two-and-a-half bundles of betel leaves. The visitors shower praise on Dhvaja while departing. "An awe-inspiring design! See the size of the windows!" they exclaim. "It's the house of a commoner with royal embellishments. Wonderful! See the gradient of the thatch."

...Champalal clowns around playing the milkman in the Gosthaleela ceremony of Bindu's son. He sings a little parody in praise of Dhvaja's workmanship, triggering a bout of laughter among the audience: "On my way back home from Vrindavan, I've seen the Tajmahal; and at Baromuni I've seen Dhvaja's Senamahal[31]. It's peerless in design and proportion."

..."Ogyaa...ogyaa...ogyaa," the new-born's first cry sounds from within the house. An overjoyed Dhvaja jumps to the

---

31 *Senamahal*: Literally 'Golden Palace' – the name of Dhvaja's house.

verandah from the courtyard in reflex action.... When he's about to go out of the main gate of his compound, the *naukalpi*[32] shouts out joyfully, "A baby boy, a baby boy!"

...Sukumal, eldest son of Dhvaja, bows down to Apokpa, the family god. He leaves home to join the army. His younger brother, Parimal, follows suit the year next. The youngest of all, Bimal, gets ready to go to college.

– "*Nirantare e e e*[33]....," the pundit sings aloud after completing a chapter of the Bhagavad Gita at a simple traditional early morning ceremony welcoming the new bride and the groom home. Sabi showers the auspicious coarse paddy grains on her eldest son, Sukumal and newly-married daughter-in-law while welcoming them. A smiling Sabi leads the bride and the groom home by holding them with both hands. Dhvaja showers blessings on the new bride, his daughter-in-law: "May you live long, lighting up this humble home..."

✻

Ka ka ka.... Crows announced the break of day with their harsh cry and rudely broke Dhvaja's reverie. It was morning. Dhvaja's heart throbbed fast. Alas! Neither Sabi, nor that sweet dream of a life, were with him. A few moments later, this home would also be.... Choked with emotion, he rubbed his eyes with the hem of the shawl. Raising his folded hands he paid homage to the departed soul of his guru Thabal, and slowly left the place.

The masons arrived with their tool bags when the sun rose higher up. Dhvaja received them in the courtyard. The young

---

32 *Naukalpi*: Midwife.

33 *Nirantare*: Keep calling God endlessly.

head mason bowed down to Dhvaja, receiving his blessings. "Live long my boy...take your seat." He pushed towards them the wooden *pirhas*[34] whittled from leftover pieces of wooden planks and moved to the cowshed.

The villagers had gathered. All household goods had been removed the day before while shifting to the cowshed as a temporary makeshift arrangement. The remaining goods were being removed now. Dhvaja's daughter-in-law was engaged in household chores after fixing Dhvaja's hubble-bubble with his morning shot of tobacco. Two old women of the village were at work, snipping betel leaves, betel nuts and banana leaves to make *pana-tankha*[35] for the occasion. Erecting the central post of the new home was a special occasion indeed, calling for a religious ritual to be held around the event. Sukumal, Parimal and Bimal were busy making small talk with the masons and other villagers in the courtyard. Sitting alone in one corner, Dhvaja simply listened to the sketchy explanation of the design of the new house given by his sons to the masons. The bowl of tobacco in his hand burned away, simmering down to dust.

"The area of the house will be 20 x 8 square cubit, with two rooms in the front, one on either side." Armyman Sukumal continued in his Hindi accent, "We have to bid the old wooden structure adieu. They have no takers nowadays. A three-inch wall will be erected on all the four sides, and the work has to be completed within two months, *jaroor.* I'm on a two-month leave, *sirf.*"

"What about the windows? Will they be of the size of the existing ones?"

---

34 *Pirha*: A low wooden seat, almost at floor-level.
35 *Pana-tankha*: Betel and areca nut for special rites.

"No, not at all. These are outdated ones. They will be four-part windows fitted with glass, about two-and-a-half feet above the floor," explained Sukumal.

"What! So low," the villagers exclaimed.

"This design is in fashion now. What I've seen in Jabalpur is even lower," he said.

"What about the kitchen?"

"It will be a muffle furnace in the rear verandah. We want to get rid of soot, completely" replied Sukumal.

"What about the traditional hearth? Perhaps there's no provision for that in the blue print."

"Certainly not."

"A hearth is too important to be left out. It's an epitaph of our housing plans," Dhvaja intervened.

Rejecting his father's proposal outright, Sukumal objected. "No, no. A round-the-clock hearth will only make the building sooty," he explained. "A hearth was a must in the days when there weren't match boxes. If need be, we will buy a stove, you know that!"

Elders and betters, as they say, have no takers. Dhvaja opted to keep silent. It was their home and only their writ would run.

..."My son, you will know the importance of a hearth at the fag-end of your life. The chilling cold of the month of Magh is fast approaching. If I need to bask in the warmth of a hearth, how can I?" Dhvaja murmured softly to himself.

Forehead and the bridge of the nose smeared with sandal paste, the village priest – the Brahmin – arrived late in a tearing hurry. "Sukumal, what are you doing?" he cried out, aghast. "First dismantle this old hulk, or else we will miss the auspicious moment for erecting the main post."

"It's an old ramshackle structure. We won't take much time to dismantle it," said Tampha, a resident of the next hamlet.

"Let's start. Where is the *eira-tankha*[36]?" the Brahmin shouted in impatience.

The villagers stood up. The mason and his helpers began preparing the mixture of cement, sand and chips for the main post. Sukumal, Parimal and Bimal, along with other villagers, climbed up the house with machetes, axes, pliers and other tools, causing Dhvaja a great deal of heartache.

...I erected this house with my own blood and sweat. Not even a single one of the houses that I erected in the village is left. They have all been replaced with new ones, terming my creations outdated...

Rising emotions caused a turmoil within Dhvaja. The best efforts in his career as a carpenter lent strength to the structures and brought forth the best designs so that his craftsmanship could live longer, even when he would be no more. The stark reality was that all these houses, his creations, had been dismantled in his lifetime and often in his presence, one after another. The only one left was his Senamahal that depicted the secret of Guru Thabal's design and strength. And none other than his scions were dismantling it today, right in front of him! Tastes changed apace! This house was the abode of his soul. If the house collapsed, he would follow suit.

They began to remove the thatch. Dhvaja heard his heart crying out: "Sukumal, Parimal, Bimal! It was your mother who lobbed weeds at me while thatching this roof. You were born and raised under this thatched house. It's that thatch under which your mother breathed her last. Aren't you ridden with guilt? Forgotten everything? So early in life!"

The clanging hammers, axes, pliers and machetes had a deafening impact on Dhvaja, whose heart was more sensitive to

---

36 *Eira-tankha*: Fruits and betel nuts for special occasions.

the sound of destruction than his ears. Each stroke of the axe or the hammer dealt a hard blow to his heart, ripping it apart. His eyes failed to hold back hot tears as they watched the demolition in progress.

"Oh! Grandpa is crying!" shouted his grand-daughter.

"Are you mad? Why should I cry?" Dhvaja scrubbed his eyes dry and smiled. In his bid to prove to his six-year-old grand-daughter and to those gathered there that he was the happiest one to get an opportunity to dwell in an RCC building, he resorted to pretence and talked incoherently with simulated enthusiasm: "Hey, Tampha, be careful. Move away... Hello, you Brahmin chap, you can select the site for the main post later on. Be careful of the loose flying wooden pieces. Hey, what-d'you-call-him... son of Tombagiri, why do you slob around? Hold the pole tight... oh...oh...oh...ouch..."

The front wall of the house collapsed with a huge bang. With all the four walls finally dismantled, only the skeletal remains of the wooden structure – hewn with his superb craftmanship – loomed over the rubble. The two damaged vertical posts, one on each side of the swinging front door, resembled the limbs of the skeleton.

The ugly scene dealt a final death blow to Dhvaja. He raised his hands, still clutching on to the staff in his right hand and cried out as loud as he could—"Oh God..."

Carpenter Dhvaja collapsed along with his house. His last and loudest cry went unheard amidst the din caused by the demolishing operation. Perhaps the departed souls of his Guru Thabal and other long-lost friends carried away the free spirit of their beloved carpenter...

Yet his eyes were fixed on the iron rods of the ceremonial post decorated with vermillion and mango leaves.... The mortal remains of octogenarian Dhvaja, widower of Sabi and father of Sukumal, Parimal and Bimal...

SEDUCING THE RAIN GOD

*K*humolmati is parched.

In the cycle of seasons, it is monsoon but one without rain. Dressing up in her erotic best, Prokriti – Mother Nature – has been waiting for Purusha, the cosmic male. Since the fourth day of Ambubachi[37], Mother Earth has been in a supine position with her eyes set on the sky. The air of Khumolmati[38] is ripe with the anticipation of Soralel, the cosmic male incarnate, who like every year, will invariably appear from the south in the guise of procreative rain clouds. This is an amorous sport that Khumolmati and Soralel annually play. What's wrong this year? No trace of clouds in the sky! An agonising wait has to be suffered by all! Khumolmati is smitten by love, and sensually aroused with a desire to unite. She takes dust in her palms, smears it on her face and body and sends it whirling in the moaning wind. Her lively and green tresses are dusty and matted. Is this a dust bath to satisfy her strong desire? Or is it her preparation for the foreplay? Dust whirls through her body pores and she resembles a poor loosely-robed mendicant Sufi 'dervish'. Is it the gloom and doom that a woman suffers when the wait for her paramour proves futile? Be that as it may, Khumolmati, otherwise blooming like a

---

37 Ambubachi: The menstrual period of Mother Earth according to Hindu mythology.
38 Khumolmati: A former independent principality of Manipur.

siroy lily[39], is burning. In the unprecedented drought; all ponds, canals, lakes and other water bodies have run dry. Fields have turned grey with dust. Even the drought-resistant *vekuri* plant has stopped flowering. The wild dusty winds have littered all households. Fields are without grass and canals without water. Livestock have been dying unnatural deaths and vultures can be spotted circling above.

The villagers dig ditches in dried ponds and canals for water. They don't think twice before drinking whatever they get. Epidemic takes its toll. A wail of despair runs through the village.

What is it that Khumolmati is paying a heavy price for?

✻

Koireng the king banished his younger brother, Chomei, from the royal court, kicking him out for daring to prevent the king from waging yet another war against Moirang, despite repeated defeats. Koireng Khullakpa[40]—Prince Chomei, had to leave Khumolmati for the Kobru hill. One of his maid servants followed him. Is this drought the punishment for the sin committed against Chomei? There's not a drop of water even in the palace. His soldiers leave for Loktak, honeypot of Khumolmati. The lake – forever frivolous and beautiful – and never lacking in water or beauty – isn't immune to the lingering dry summer fallout.

"Alas! What does life hold in store for us?" Koireng asks his soldiers. "Go, and bring a woman who can seduce the rain god, Soralel. Invite her. The thirst of Khumolmati won't be quenched unless a rainmaker appeases Soralel."

---

39 Siroy lily: The state flower of Manipur.
40 *Koireng Khullakpa*: A crown prince.

The soldiers now leave, not for water, but for a woman skilled in the art of 'rainmaking'.

*

Sabi, a plain woman of forty, isn't sure whether she's a deserted wife or a widow. Her husband, who left for Cachar with Maharaj Kalaraja as a soldier, hasn't returned. She can't remember the exact date of his parting. He left when their son was a toddler. Is he a fallen hero? Has he married again? Sabi knows nothing. She, however, is waiting for him, counting her days. Hers is an unending wait. The drought in her womb is far more acute than that of Khumolmati. In conformity with the menstrual cycle, she menstruates, but her desire remains unsatisfied. She resides on a *phumdi*[41] that has no legal owner. As personal possession, she has only Tampha, her son. Tampha is growing fast. Now he can row a boat between *phumdi*s, catch fish, take dips in Loktak and emerge with water lilies. But Sabi's youthful face has a pallor, her curvaceous body looks stricken. Regardless of age, the woman has a heavy cross to bear, especially on moonlit nights when she stares gloomily at the choppy waters of the lake, her hideout. She doesn't seem to be quite herself at night. Her body and mind get excited; they only calm down the next morning. When she mournfully strokes her taut, concave abdomen with her hands, her sultry sighs waft across the lake, only to return and lose themselves in the harsh reality of life. Making both ends meet is more than a tough task for her. Come rain, come shine; she has to collect arum rhizome and other edible plants from the banks of the lake.

---

41 *Phumdi*: A floating biomass found in Loktak Lake.

The troopers of Koireng come to Sabi's *phumsang*[42], followed
by yokels in hordes. "Koireng's army!" Sabi, quite taken aback,
returns sharply. "What's up? Anything wrong! Any message?"
Tampha... O...Tampha, my darling; hurry up! Where have
you gone? Koireng's troopers are here."

One of the soldiers alights from the horse, bows down before
Sabi and conveys Koireng's appeal to her with e*ira-tankha*[43].

"Khumolmati is burning. The drought is spelling doom for
the nation. You're a proven rainmaker of the present times.
Save the nation from this killer drought with the most exclusive
knowledge at your command."

A request or an order from Koireng; it means the same to
Sabi. She has an impeccable record in 'rainmaking'. Her efforts for
appeasing Soralel have never failed. She doesn't have an inch of
land in the field of Khumolmati. She's however, proud to be part
of a nation, and serve her duty towards the same. She has learnt
the art of 'rainmaking' from her forefathers for the well-being of
people. Sabi graciously accepts the invitation. The elated sepoys
depart and so does the crowd.

*

Since the early hours of next day, a growing apprehension keeps
haunting Sabi. Soralel has never failed to respond to an appeal
from a nude Sabi at the dead of night. However, there's no room for
complacency because of this unfailing track record. Sabi's anxiety
stems from the apprehension of the consequences if it doesn't
rain despite her best efforts. What will be the fate of the King's

42 *Phumsang*: A cottage erected on a *phumdi*.
43 *Eira-tankha*: Ceremonial offering of fruits and betel nuts.

order and the hopes and aspirations of the people? With her hands folded, she prays: "Oh Soralel, shower mercy on me as you always do. Don't let me down. Be kind to the people of Khumolmati."

Rising above the Chinkhei Hill, the sun proudly proclaims triumph over darkness on the eastern horizon. Sabi starts the job of cherry-picking the women well-versed in the songs and dances of 'rainmaking'. She gets a warm reception wherever she goes.

"Oh, Soralel, don't let me down," she prays again. Back home at noon, she gets busy with a long-drawn bath. The effects of using aromatic *chengi*[44] as hair conditioner and *khar*[45] made out of burnt banana husk as body cleanser are quite visible, having added a special sheen to her glowing skin. A post-lunch beauty nap renders her physically and mentally fit and relaxed to spend a sleepless night out.

Tampha goes boating again while Sabi remains busy with household chores till evening.

"Hey Ima[46], I'm hungry. Give me some rice," says Tampha while sponging his body with a towel. He has moored the boat and propped the oar against the reed-wall of their phumsang. Tampha strongly resembles his father with his crop of curly hair, an obtrusive nose and a raincloud-dark complexion. His tender muscles – yet to reach their final masculine shape – do however, hold promise of sturdiness. A growing boy, Tampha frequently suffers hunger pangs and rushes to his biological mother only when he's hungry. He feels comfortable spending the rest of his time with his other mother, the Loktak lake.

---

44 *Chengi*: A traditional hair conditioner comprising water used in washing uncooked rice and some aromatic herbs of special fragnance.

45 *Khar*: An alkaline solution used as detergent.

46 *Ima*: Mother.

"Ima, I'm too hungry," he says.

"Wait, wait. Rice isn't fast food. It has to be cooked. Have this stuff now." Sabi serves a small snack between meals – a boiled edible root and two brood fruits – on a broad round leaf of the lily plant. The fragrance of chengi hits Tampha's nostrils. He stares bemusedly at his mother. Her tresses shine and dance, making mild waves. Tampha notices a divine beauty in his mother.

"Ima! You look very beautiful," Tampha says with a tinge of admiration. "Why have you dressed specially?"

"I haven't yet, but I will after serving you your meal. The onus is on me to propitiate the Rain God today. Koireng invited me yesterday. Don't you remember?" she reminds him.

Tampha still has his eyes set on his mother's lustrous tresses that almost reach her knees.

"Why don't you dress this way, everyday?"

"Woo hoo!" The loud hoot was the only response from Sabi.

A tired Tampha gobbles his food down to the last morsel. He falls asleep in no time.

✻

Sabi keeps a lamp in the middle of the cottage, brings the big copper plate that she once used to serve her husband food, fills it with water and makes a water mirror ready. She looks at herself mirrored in the plateful of clear water. With a buffalo-horn comb, she starts untangling her knotted hair. She wears a high bun balanced and kept in place by a porcupine spike. A pair of dangling marigolds in her ears adds to her charm. Her fawn eyes look even more enchanting when she lines their edges with lamp-black; even Sabi loses herself in her own charm while staring at her reflection. When dressed in a traditional outfit –

a faded red *angaluri*[47] and a snow-white *inafi*[48] – she looks extremely elegant. She has no parallel, not even among other younger, pretty lasses.

"Tampha's father, poor guy, you've missed this look," Sabi thinks, incredulous about her own maturing beauty. Bowing down to Pahangpa and Soralel, she leaves for the assigned task. Looking back at her sleeping son, she feels sorry as he too has missed seeing her in her finery. Closing the half-door of the phumsang, she steps out, looking like a white flower blooming by the roadside amidst dusty leaves. The lamplit phumsangs in the lake and their gleaming images in the water remind her of Diwali nights. Giving the responsibility to look after Tampha to her neighbour Taraleima, she walks up to the bank of the lake. Some women from Khangabok and Hairok join her with fishing devices—a number of bamboo traps.

The residents of Khumolmati, including Koireng, have been waiting for Sabi with baited breath. Attired in a dhoti, an angabastra and a *fizang*[49], Koireng stands under the royal umbrella. His troopers stand like statues, so do the horses near them. The ambience is steeped in silence fraught with anxiety. Spotting their favourite rainmaker and her troupe approach, the gathering turns jovial. They offer the group a warm reception amidst plenty of cheering! A confused Sabi glances at Koireng and bows down before him. Accepting the veneration, Koireng says, "You are generosity personified, coupled with an unbeatable record in seducing the Rain God. Please, save Khumolmati. The odds are that you can do it. If you can't, I'll have no place to live in, not even in hell."

---

47 A*ngaluri*: A traditional Bishnupriya Manipuri lower garment for women.
48 *Inafi*: A traditional Bishnupriya Manipuri shawl for women.
49 *Fizang*: A traditional Bishnupriya Manipuri white round turban.

Repentance is like a hot blazing inferno which burns and simmers in the mind, without throwing up sparks.

With the blessing of Koireng, Sabi says, "Your Highness, I'm at your command." She and her troupe leave for the paddy field. A few women from the capital too join them. Unable to beat the killer drought, an otherwise mighty and wealthy king has no alternative but to pin all hopes on the woman brigade, his last resort.

The field begins where the village ends. The women take fistfuls of dust from the field and smear it on their foreheads. Leading from the front is Sabi. The onlookers watch them. A few young girls – virgins all of them – street-smart though, and fashionable with fringed sleek hair, follow the group. The elders, however, call them back. "Why have you been following them?"

"We want to see how the Rain God is appeased."

"It's forbidden for virgins. A divine ordain."

"Let's go and see how the rite is performed," a few young and immature boys come forward.

"No, males are totally barred, regardless of age."

"Why?"

"Grow up first to have access to all such information."

They soon gave up on the hopes of their adventure of the unknown, but not their inquisitiveness on Soralel. Why is it forbidden? How does Soralel come? What does he do? They start painting a rosy picture of Soralel, much to the elders' amusement.

*

Sabi and the women set off for the field and gradually vanish under the cloak of dust and haze. The field and the air are hot, even at this late hour of night. As soon as they find the coast clear, their clothes come off and the middle-aged women experience an arousal, enjoying their vibrant sexuality, stirred by the dormant sexual fervour in their nude bodies, their repressed minds tasting a rare freedom that night. The free feminine ambience in the dark makes them giggle and frolic like young adolescent girls out on blind dates. They start cracking jokes spiced with sexual inuendos, all of them targeted at Sabi.

"Why is Sabi *gidei*[50] in such a tearing hurry?" they casually banter, eyeing and nudging each other.

"She knows that He'll come now. Watch her movements. She'll **** without fail," the women adept at comical acts take another amorous dig at Sebi.

"You naughty girls, why are you so noisy and talkative? Mind your tongue, don't let it go so loose!"

"Oh, but why should we do that? We'll watch everything tonight and feast our eyes on what we see."

"But what is that?" Sabi softly retorts.

"Oh! What a classic pretence!" They lightly embrace her and titter in sensuous tones.

Oh Rain God, cause a downpour.

❊

They stop in the middle of the field, look around and make sure that there's none to see them. Sabi arranges all the material for the secret and sacred rite on a banana leaf. She offers eira-tankha, lights a *vartika*[51] and begins her ode to Soralel. When the vartika goes out, all of them lie prone on the ground. Sabi rises with a song pleading Soralel to cause a downpour:

---

50 *Gidei*: A salutation addressing an elder sister.
51 *Vartika*: A lamp.

Soralelte Rajaro, leipak pungou koilo
Leipake marai makhonge, khoimu e jangal dilo
Khumolor mati hukeilo, boron diyade douraja
Lu-kom mahi nukulil, boron diyade douraja.

(Oh Rain God, put an end to the killer drought in Khumolmati with a
downpour...)

All other women join in the chorus. With their hands raised above
their heads, they start calling out to Soralel. In her melodious
voice, Sabi paints a vivid picture of the plight of the people of
Khumolmati. At the end of each verse she chants a prayer for a
downpour, followed by a chorus:

"The people of Khumolmati have given up eating and
drinking. Who will eat in such a situation? What's left there to
eat and drink? The land has turned into hell and death looms
large at every doorstep. Oh Soralel, come in the form of clouds
to this land of death, and sprinkle your procreative blessings as a
downpour to bring in birth and life."

The villagers have been waiting with drums and cymbals to
welcome Soralel. Looking up at the clear sky, they find no trace
of clouds. Sabi sings on: "Repentance has kept Koireng under a
boiling furnace. The injustice meted out to Chomei doesn't let
him die, nor does it allow him to live in peace. Merrymaking in
Khumolmati is a thing of the past. The people have sacrificed
all joy at the feet of Pahangpa. They've followed the footsteps
of Birobahu, son of Ravana, to rid themselves of sin. Laxmana
had to pardon Birobahu only because of self-purification. Oh,
Pahangpa's father Soralel, come in the form of clouds and
sprinkle your procreative waters. Let the deluge wash all sins
away. Oh Soralel, be kind and cause a downpour." The chorus
follows Sabi's prayer.

Sabi describes to Soralel the series of incidents that have led to the unprecedented drought in Khumolmati and the story of the curse leading to the Ganga being held midway down her course, not being allowed to continue with her natural flow downstream. Staring at the clear night sky, Sabi's eyes well up with tears. Her appeal has never gone in vain. Soralel has always been responsive to her. Why has he turned a deaf ear to her call today? What's wrong with her? Choked with emotion, she's unable to sing. Her backup singers just keep the chorus going on. Clearing her voice, Sabi starts singing again...

"His Holiness Pahangpa has every reason to sulk at the ill-treatment meted out to Khullakpa Chomei by Koireng. Troops have been sent to bring Chomei back. Though Chomei and Beti are hesitant to return, the troopers are bringing their second daughter back home. All arrangements have been made to welcome her with many gifts. Oh Soralel, appease His Holiness Pahangpa and cause a downpour." The chorus follows.

Clouds are seen nowhere in the sky, nor is there any sign of imminent inclement weather. Though there's no visible lapse in Sabi's devotion, her efforts seem to have gone in vain. Sabi flops down on the ground. With a broken heart, she continues to sing huskily, finally breaking down and weeping, along with her mates. The chorus however, manages to keep the song going with clockwork precision, keeping the main motif of the ritual – 'Cause a downpour, O Soralel'– alive.

*

A cool breeze mildly fragrant of rainclouds starts blowing gently, closely followed by lightning and thunder.

"Soralel is here! He's here!" The women are stirred out of their sad stupor all of a sudden and they start shouting in excitement, as though struck by lightning. The piece of dark cloud makes its joyous appearance from the southern sky, flexing his strong muscles. Watching the dark clouds approach from the Cachar skies, Sabi loses herself in the vision, laughing and crying at the same moment. Overwhelmed and with her emotions running high, she dances with her head rolling all around, her dishevelled hair flying in all directions. Other women simply follow her motions, leaving Soralel in a dilemma. Over twenty beautiful, nude women dance seductively at a fast pace, their hair neatly rolled and knotted high – studded with marigolds – with Sabi leading them:

Choha jura badho, senarei pidiya nacho
Choha jura badhohe Moirang leirir tole homailo.

(Wear high buns studded with marigold and dance. Wear high buns, and see that Moirang has gone under a steep slope).

Having savoured the exotic spectacle of nude seducers dancing elegantly to appease him, the lustful Rain God Soralel turns north. The dance and the tune of the song slow down to a soulful hum. Sabi's eyes brim with tears again. "*Hiliri beelor pohonchaka Uda kene alo jarga!*"

The women let their hair down to hold Soralel back in the Land of Loktak with his nectar, before gliding on to another direction. Sabi's hair tumbles down her bare back in a dark cascade; her warm tears drench her silken locks. The women dance to a soulful tune, pleading "Oh Soralel, cause a downpour".

Sabi's vocal prowess surpasses that of others and appears to hold back Soralel, the Casanova. All women call out to Soralel with their hands raised high. Soralel perhaps notices the beautiful sultry Sabi—hands raised and eyes tearful. She's a known face, the great hope among rainmakers! Soralel stops and turns to look at her.

*

Joy spreads in the air. Sabi and her backup singers realise that it's going to rain, without fail. They resume their dance with a fresh vigour:

Udai dilo tingla tala
Pahuri ghore beli ahilu
Battiye ali karere maze changninge
Kochur pate nabadher liklaro sena meichamore.

The bare-bodied women start a dance aping the farmers. They pretend as if they have forgotten to carry *talas*[52] to shield their sacred bodies from the all-pervasive, lascivious eyes of Soralel and his sharp, penetrating droplets. A woman, pretending to be a midget farmer, Batti, uproots saplings from the nursery bed and ties them in bundles. Untying one of the bundles, Sabi discovers a fresh droplet of water shining like a bead of gold hidden in the saplings. At the sight of this sacred, procreative water droplet gifted by Soralel the Rain God, Sabi appears to go crazy in joy. In due course, more such droplets will impregnate the paddy plants of Khumolmati.

With both the hands up, Sabi sings: "Oh Soralel, cause a heavy downpour..."

Khumolmati – returning to its primordial roots – performs erotic nocturnal rituals involving over twenty mature and vivacious women joyfully celebrating their nudity and sexuality, dancing with their full breasts held high and their curvaceous thighs bending into erotic poses to welcome procreation and new life on earth. Sabi moves her head in a frenzy, dancing and singing like a woman possessed! Soralel, taken aback by such a

---

52 *Tala*: A traditional head gear made of palm leaves used by farmers.

show of erotica, is perhaps apprehensive of making advances and takes a few halting steps but Sabi is too determined and knowledgeable a seductress. She does not let the cloud from the Cachar hills leave her unnoticed and changes into frenzied but irresistible dancing. Moments later, dense clouds envelop the sky and gaze down lovingly at Sabi. Her body, smeared with dust, speaks its own language. And the dark saturated clouds start pouring down...drop by drop...as the much-awaited rain over Khumolmati while Sabi is lost in her own vision of a passionate lover – her long-lost soldier in Cachar – kissing, fondling and making love, throwing her into orgasmic gasps of pleasure.

Rainwater flows down her deep cleavage like a hill stream, fuming and bubbling around her deep, dry belly button—the proverbial 'honey-pot' of procreation and new life. The other women too lie relaxed and satiated. The clouds have melted and penetrated deep into the womb of Khumolmati. The parched earth too, begins to melt. Thus Khumolmati's ceaseless wait for the Rain God's blessings comes to an end, at long last.

Sabi opens her eyes slowly and the other women start a *jolokeli*[53], splashing muddy water on her bare body. Far off, the villagers including Koireng, beat drums and cymbals.

Sensing the approach of dawn with the rising chorus, the women cover their bodies with their wet clothes and start walking home, giggling. Rippling, gurgling rainwater cascading down the hill troughs and the fields are also bound for Loktak.

In the village, they receive a hero's welcome. A drenched but joyous Koireng leaves the *sekpil*[54] and welcomes the victorious women. Sabi and her colleagues bow down before the stunned

---

53 *Jolokeli*: Water sport.
54 *Sekpil*: A royal umbrella.

king. His eyes look at Sabi with immense gratitude and praise writ large.

"Thank you, and thanks to your supernatural wisdom. Blessed by Soralel, you've saved me and my people. What honorarium befits you? A hint please?"

Shying away from the limelight and the clamour building around her, a dumbstruck Sabi just hangs her head. Koireng repeats his generous offer. The women have their eyes fixed on Sabi. The king is oblivious of the fact that Sabi is a landless grass widow.

"Now, money will roll in! She'll demand a lot of gold and silver ornaments or even half the kingdom," the women whisper excitedly to each other. The king is waiting for Sabi to voice her demand. In the heavy shower, rain water flows down her tresses and face through her cleavage. She pulls the inafi closer to her body and doesn't move, nor utters a single word.

"If Sabi sets her demand right, the king won't even hesitate to accept her as a concubine," one of her colleagues remarks. They whisper to Sabi: "Raise your demand right. Fully avail this heaven-sent opportunity! Don't you see, the king is so elated today? Even if you demand a berth in his bedroom, he won't hesitate to meet that. You and your son can live a comfortable and lavish life—royal treatment, food, clothes..."

Sabi looks at her colleagues. Writhing with embarrassment, she makes an attempt to speak, only to keep silent again after an eye contact with the king.

"Tell me. Don't hesitate," the king reassures her.

"Your Highness; you're the king, our father. Propitiating the Rain God isn't my profession. This supernatural erudition percolates down generations. It's a public knowledge for public welfare. It's my duty towards the nation. Charging honourarium for such a sacred service is a sin; it is forbidden. That makes the traditional knowledge less effective," she says.

Sabi's reply takes Koireng and others by surprise. A stunned Koireng says, "I'm very pleased with your judgment and line of thinking. You've played your part to save the nation. If not honourarium, as the king, I've a duty to reward you. Just tell me, what can I do for you?"

"Your Highness, I don't want anything else. My only problem is that my husband went to Cachar as a soldier of Maharaj Kalaraja, long back. He hasn't returned as yet. I only want to know where and how he is.... I'll be at your service for this benevolence." Sabi breaks down, and falls on the king's feet.

"Oh lady, don't cry. If he's alive, I'll bring him back to you. It's my promise. You may rest assured that I'll do all I can to find him. Go home now," the king says.

*

Sabi turns homeward, splashing through the muddy water. Her friends rebuke her: "You foolish woman! You live in cloud cuckoo land. You don't even own a piece of land to live in. You could have demanded at least some land and a house!"

Sabi and her colleagues are different from each other as chalk from cheese. Their words fail to reach her ears that ring with the king's ringing promise – "I'll bring him back...I'll bring him back... I'll bring him back." As though enriched by a long-lost treasure, Sabi firmly strides through the field overflowing with rain water and the reproach of her friends go unheeded.

*

Her bosom heaving and short of breath, Sabi flops down on the bank of the Loktak. The downpour continues. Fed with the rainwater, the lake – the proverbial honey-pot of Khumolmati

– swells up fast. Sabi realises that, be it late, Mother Earth has been 'impregnated'. Brisk preparations for the great process of procreation in nature are visible everywhere. Leipirik, Dharampushpa and other herbs start germinating. A miserable Sabi heaves a deep, doleful sigh. Massaging her concave abdomen, she looks at the array of clouds bound for Cachar. Tears roll down her cheeks. She's miles away from her beloved.

Suddenly she remembers Tampha and jumps up. She had left him alone, fast asleep. What could the poor child's plight be in this sudden, heavy downpour? With much apprehension she rushes back home. The roof of the thatched house has been blown away. And the door has swung wide open. She steps in gingerly. It never rains but it pours in her home. The floor is full of the water dripping from above. A sulking Tampha sits in a corner of the house, wrapped up in a shawl. He's drenched to his skin. Sabi squeezes out her inafi and sponges Tampha's head with that.

"Why have you invited this downpour? Since you've brought in the bane for us, tackle it yourself now," a glum Tampha complains. Uttering not a word, Sabi simply starts piling up all household goods. The water level rises fast, about to cross their threshold. Tampha too joins his mother and starts loading household goods onto his boat. Finally they set off in their boat. Barely a few minutes later, their phumsang too goes down under the surging water. Amidst the downpour, with Tampha handling the boat, Sabi is on the lookout for a virgin phumdi—their new shelter for the rainy days ahead.

LILAVATI

*K*ut...kut...kut ta...kut...kut...

Lilavati, the eight-year-old young virgin child deserted by her playmates, is playing hopscotch. She's marked hopscotch squares in the courtyard, eight in number, with a broken flat piece from an earthen pitcher. Throwing the piece to each and every square in succession, she hops from one square to another, and marks X in each square, after every successful round of hopping. With each hop, her long lock of hair dances, making waves, and so do her earrings. The small towel she is clad in as an *angaluri*[55] has been hitched up to her knees. She has her chest covered with a *yaberuni,*[56] tied in a loose knot at the back. Kut...kut...kut...

The family temple stands in the northeast side of the courtyard facing the south with a small *mandapa*[57] in the front. Just behind the courtyard, there's a thatched clay house with flowering plants and the sacred *tulsi* – the basil plant – resembling a hermitage. Seated in the classic cross-legged *padmasana* posture on a low-raised floor couch (a traditional *golisarfita*[58] in Bishnupuriya Manipuri) is Bhaskaracharya, Lilavati's father. The verandah

---

55 *Angaluri*: An indigenously woven Bishnupriya Manipuri lower garment for women.

56 *Yaberuni*: An indigenously woven Bishnupriya Manipuri brassiere.

57 *Mandapa*: A covered traditional community hall for local community meetings, festivities and religious functions.

58 *Golisarfita*: An indigenously woven seat of honour.

has been rubbed clean and sanctified with a viscous mix of cowdung and clay. Enlightened from within, Bhaskaracharya has a beaming face with a quill-like sharp nose set between the deep blue pools of his eyes—resembling the inkpot at his feet. With two streaks of *chandan*[59] running vertically down the forehead, a tonsured head sporting a long tuft of hair at the back and a chain of dried basil seeds around the neck—Bhaskaracharya is a symbol of sanctity. An authority on mathematics and philosophy, he does not accept any conclusion or theory without adequate proof, which is why his books are looked upon with great regard everywhere in the country, even beyond the territory of his workplace, the holy city of Ujjain. The accurate calculation and the almost magical determination of the accurate movement of stars, their shapes and characteristics has put Bhaskaracharya where he is today among all astronomers. Now he's busy writing a book comprising new conclusive decisions on mathematics, on the *bhurjapatra*[60]. A few of the initial chapters are already over. Verses of theorems follow one after the other.

Bhaskaracharya raises his head and glances at Lilavati. The girl is engaged in playing hopscotch, all alone. Bereft of maternal love at a tender age, she is a little naughty, rather innocent and easily breaks into tears. Bringing up a girl child single-handedly by the father is a serious matter. He goes back to writing the mathematical formulae. A giggling Lilavati starts clapping in delight when the piece of clay settles down clean on the particular square she has aimed it at. Bhaskaracharya raises his head and looks at his daughter again. The courtyard – once bubbling with

---

59 *Chandan*: Sandalwood paste, commonly used for religious purposes and for drawing auspicious marks on the nosebridge and forehead of Brahmins. Also for bridal make-up in eastern India.
60 *Bhurjapatra*: The broad and hardy leaves of the Himalayan Birch – close to the Beech or Oak family – used in ancient India for writing scriptures. It is a Sanskrit term.

children playing hopscotch, crying and quarrelling – wears a deserted look now, barring the clapping and giggling by the lone Lilavati in the course of her play.

Other close friends of Lilavati have been recently married off, one after another. Marriage at such an early age does not sound very reasonable to Bhaskaracharya! This is the custom of a society with scant regard for reason. At this age, neither does the mind develop, nor the body. Let Lilavati grow up first. Besides, Lilavati is his only daughter. Apprehension of imminent loneliness haunts Bhaskaracharya, though he is aware that this cannot stand in the way of her marriage. However, marriage at such an early age is inconceivable. His mind and conscience at constant war with each other, Bhaskaracharya keeps himself busy all day evolving mathematical formulae. Time passes by. Bhurjapatras containing principles and theorems of mathematics pile up. The innumerable scars on the earthen floor of the verandah standing as glaring proof to his formulae are erased every morning while sweeping and plastering the floors with a fresh swab of clay and cowdung-water.

Bhaskaracharya is well aware of community codes and the infamy that growing unmarried daughters are subjected to. The community is not full of scholars and sensible people! The mass is mostly an illiterate lot. All playmates of Lilavati have been married. Bhaskaracharya's community frowns upon the father's reluctance and negligence in getting his daughter married.

*

One day, Lilavati draws Bhaskaracharya's attention while playing hopscotch alone. The scene causes Bhaskaracharya much heartache. Putting the quill and the bhurjapatra down, he ponders about his daughter's fate.

Bhaskaracharya detests the growing grumblings among his neighbours and friends. Word goes around in whispers. *Why is he evasive when it comes to his daughter's marriage? His daughter is a lass of eight years now—and a spinster! So engrossed is this man in his calculations on planetary movements that he has no time to look at his growing daughter? Is he reluctant to marry her off? Or is he on the lookout for a match where the boy is ready to be a live-in son-in-law?*

Bhaskaracharya doesn't heed the ramblings of the common folk. Let his daughter remain unmarried. He too loves and respects a disciplined society and social codes, barring the unreasonable customs. All his research work is geared towards the well-being of society. He too respects his discoveries and inventions, which have helped him hold his head high. He has the strength to fight an uncompromising battle against dogmas and superstitions. But, why should the budding blossom – his only child Lilavati – fade away and have no future due to her father's stubbornness?

Spinster! At the age of eight! Utter rubbish! Mere incoherent utterances of a sick society. On the other hand, it was true that he himself had grown old and had begun to feel his age. In the event of his death, who would look after his daughter? Where was a safe shelter for a lonely unmarried girl in this society?

Bhaskaracharya is entrapped in a dilemma—a raging conflict brews between the rational scientist and the responsible father of a motherless daughter. While the scientist is against any compromise on irrational social codes, the father can't sit at ease when his innocent and only daughter treads a path, leading her nowhere.

"After coming of age, if she asks me as to why I haven't arranged her marriage at the right age, how shall I answer her? Which does weigh more—my logic or her future? Had Lilavati's mother been alive, she would have surely arranged something."

"You're quite a lost soul, Father. What's up? Any problem in the calculation? I'm here to help you out," the tender voice of Lilavati rings out clear. Bhaskaracharya had been unaware of the little girl's close presence.

"Come on. Let's play hopscotch," Lilavati holds her father's hand and pulls him. He willfully accompanies her.

Bhaskaracharya girds up his loincloth, uses the cloth that wraps his body as the waistband, and lobs the broken slab to a square. He starts hopping—kut...kut...kut. Accidentally, one of his feet touches the line of a square. By the rules of the game, his turn is no longer alive. Clapping in delight, Lilavati starts giggling; so does Bhaskaracharya. The neighbours too, enjoy the scene.

What fate ordains

Gauging the gravity of the situation, Bhaskaracharya puts on hold his research and gets down to the serious business of finding a suitable match for Lilavati. Clad in dhoti-kurta with a snow-white shawl woven with indigenously-spun cotton thrown over his shoulders as a frill, shod in a pair of wooden clogs and an umbrella strung from his shoulder, Bhaskaracharya sets out every morning with a prayer on his lips for good luck, only to return home in the evening, dejected and frustrated. Is there any dearth of a good match for the only daughter of the famous Bhaskaracharya in Ujjain? Who in Ujjain wouldn't want to get Lilavati as his daughter-in-law? Had Bhaskaracharya given up his rigid stand against early marriage at least two years back, he could have arranged even a *svayamver*[61]. It's too late now. All probable matches for

61 *Svayamver*: A ceremony allowing a maiden to choose her match herself from prospective grooms.

Lilavati have already got married. Not a single probable groom of her age group remains. A beaming Bhaskaracharya leaving every morning and returning dejected in the evening doesn't escape the notice of his caring daughter.

"Father, is anything wrong? Where do you go everyday?"

Bhaskaracharya, a man of few words, dawdles for a while. At last, he bares his soul to her: "My darling, you have grown up now. It's time for your marriage. I'm on the lookout for a match for you."

"Marriage!" Lilavati is stunned.

"Yes," answers Bhaskaracharya.

"Oh good! I'll get a playmate! It's so boring having to play hopscotch alone! But he will be a boy. So be it," an elated Lilavati starts thinking and planning accordingly.

From then onwards, whenever her father returned home frustrated, she asked him without fail, "Father, have you found any bridegroom today?"

The only reply that came from the poor father everyday was, "No, not yet."

Now the gnawing anxiety of Lilavati grows in serious proportions. With the visible change in Bhaskaracharya's demeanour, his neighbours too begin to extend a helping hand in getting a suitable match for Lilavati.

One day a proposal comes through one of the neighbours. Like every other day, Bhaskaracharya leaves home in the morning but returns early. Reading the beaming face of his father right, Lilavati questions, "Father, have you found one?"

"Yes, my darling. I've found one, the only son of an astrologer, Gagan Shastri, living in a far-flung village. The boy seems to be a good-mannered lad. He's twelve. At this age, he has completed *vyakarana*[62] and started *nyayashastra*[63] in the *chatuspathi*[64] of Shastriji."

"Do you think this boy can play hopscotch? Does he play the make-believe bridegroom?"

"You know, he wants to study mathematics."

"How many playing pots does he have?"

"I've got a match of my choice for you. You will lead a happy life."

"Tell me first, which does he like more—the tales of kings and queens or those of demons?"

"He can do everything. But you're preoccupied with games and fairytales. Don't you want to study a bit of mathematics?"

"Okay. I will give him my clay bird. What's his name? When will he come?"

"They have agreed to everything, but set a condition that the horoscopes have to match. Your mother had prepared your horoscope with the help of an astrologer."

"Father, please tell me, when will he come?"

"If everything goes as planned, the wedding shall be held on the eleventh day of the lunar month."

"Why haven't you brought him along with you today?"

She then starts counting seventh, eighth, ninth, tenth, eleventh...on her finger tips.

On the scheduled day, Bhaskaracharya takes out the horoscope of Lilavati from a *japi*[65]. Everything in store for Lilavati is written in it. In the morning light, Baskaracharya opens the

---

62 *Vyakarana*: Grammar.

63 *Nyayashastra*: The science of logic.

64 *Chatuspathi*: Primary level village school teaching Vedas, Puranas and Shastras.

65 *Japi*:A bamboo basket.

horoscope. He looks at the *chhak*[66] first, followed by the zodiac, planets, stars etc. Astrology and astronomy sound alike, and their terminologies seem to be one; but the mode of calculation, results and interpretations are quite different. He fails to read the horoscope correctly. Bhaskaracharya rolls the horoscope and leaves for the house of Gagan Shastri, along with some of his neighbours. This is an astrologer's job, not his.

Shastri-ji is busy teaching his son out in the courtyard. Seated on a *kushasan*, his son is reading Sanskrit verses with a perfect pronunciation, singing them out in a melodious voice. With his eyes closed, Shastri-ji listens to the recitation. Bhaskaracharya throws an affectionate glance at the boy—he appears very keen to acquire knowledge. Shastri-ji receives him warmly and offers him a seat. His son bows to the guests and leaves. A good boy! After the formal introduction, the two men come to the vital point. The boy then starts practising verses inside the house. Bhaskaracharya hands over the horoscope to Shastri-ji.

Pandit Gagan reads the horoscope—born during *shuklapakshya, tula rashi, gan debari...*

Bhaskaracharya, on the other hand, loses himself in the sweet recitation of verses. A wave of affection inundates his heart, his entire being. He takes a trip down memory lane...the boy reading verses changes into a young Bhaskaracharya and the teacher into his father Maheswaracharya, master of the four Vedas.

With a distinct frown, Shastri-ji's face turns stony, much to the utter surprise of others.

"Acharya-ji!"

Bhaskaracharya comes to his senses, and replies, "Yes, please."

---

66 *Chhak*: A blue print.

"You are a leading light in all shastras. We aren't in your league. You should have gone through this horoscope yourself first."

"Pardon?"

"Who else can calculate planetary movement as accurately as you can? You should have calculated it yourself." Shastriji hands over the horoscope to the astronomer.

"I know about shapes and nature of stars and planets, their accurate measurement and calculation on them; but I know nothing about astrology that deals with the influence of stars and planets on human life. That doesn't come under the scope of astronomy. That's not my domain. Would you please tell me your findings?"

"This marriage isn't possible." An almost settled marriage hits an astrological roadblock.

"A widowed life is in store for your daughter," the astrologer predicts in a stern voice.

All those present are dumbstruck, and the sweet recitation sounds discordant at this moment. A stunned Bhaskaracharya carefully checks the horoscope and questions the pundit in a stern voice, "Any proof?"

"An ocular proof is possible only after marriage. I do have a wish to have an intelligent girl as my daughter-in-law, but that doesn't mean that I need to expose my only son to the jaws of death. What's ordained by fate is inevitable."

How can one's events in life be predicted? The decision of providence is destiny. What's providence? How to search destiny? An inner strife makes Bhaskaracharya restless. Not knowing what to do and how to react, he asks Gagan-ji, "Pandit-ji, do ominous signals have their influence on the lives of women only? Don't they have anything to do on the lives of men, predicting the life of a widower? Do all these calculations and predictions have any basis?"

"Acharya-ji, life isn't arithmetic. Astrology dates back to the ancient times. It's a scripture from our forefathers. I've just spelt out what astrology says. A debate on this will lead us nowhere. You're my guest, and I hope you will bear with me."

As the matter takes an unwanted turn, others accompanying Bhaskaracharya quickly intervene:

"Wait...wait! Esteemed scholars, please restrain yourselves. The life of an innocent girl is in your hands. Acharya-ji, we don't feel like reminding you of the responsibility of a girl's father. Pandit-ji, certainly there will be a remedy for the ominous signal of widowhood. You're an astrologer of repute. Please find an astrological remedy for it," one of them says.

A restrained Shastri-ji knits his eyebrows together and reads the horoscope afresh. Bhaskaracharya, on the other hand, keeps silent. He raises his head and notices the boy standing near the door and looking at him with an innocent smile playing on his lips. He stops reading the verses. Bhaskaracharya has to respond to him by pushing out a smile.

"Oh yes, there's a remedy," Pandit Gagan raises his head up and prescribes, "If the marriage can be conducted at the *tritiya danda* of *prathama prahara*[67], the ominous signal will have no impact. Acharya-ji, your opinion please!"

"What else is there to say? When Pundit-ji has prescribed the remedy, we better accept it." Bhaskaracharya keeps silent. Silence gives consent.

"Before handing over the girl ceremonially, we have to perform a rite. A growing banana plant, eight *ghat*[68]s, a red cloth, red flowers, betelnuts and *dubari* herbs are a must for it. The girl has to be married to the banana plant first, and then to the boy exactly at the *tritiya danda* of *prathama prahara*," the pundit spells out.

----

67 *Tritiya danda* of *prathama prahara*: The segment of time between the 48th and the 72nd moment of the early morning hours (6 am to 9 am is pratham prahar and each danda is of 24 moments).

68 *Ghat*: Small metal pot with a round, stout bottom; a *lota* in Hindi.

Marriage with a banana plant! What kind of a remedy is this? Bhaskaracharya finds no basis of this tradition.

"Acharya-ji, it's time to finalise," one of the old men says.

"Pandit-ji, I'll keep all materials ready, but you will have to perform the rite yourself. That's above my knowledge and reasoning. Calculating the right moment for the ceremonial handing over of the bride is my responsibility. May we now part on a positive note?" Bhaskaracharya asks with his hands folded. He rises, and so do his companions.

Pundit Gagan nods and gives them a warm send-off, with hands folded. He hints his son to bow down to them. The lad quietly obeys.

"Live long and be wise, my boy," an elated Bhaskaracharya wishes him.

Sandy moments of life

Everything is ready on the penultimate day of the wedding. Lilavati can't wait to show off her wedding finery to the neighbours. Bhaskaracharya, on the other hand, keeps all the material required for the ceremony closely guarded in a corner of the temple for warding off the ominous signal. He sits in front of the deities with two neatly washed earthen pitchers. At the bottom of one of the pitchers he pricks a tiny hole. He brings very carefully sieved and dried sand comprising only the finer particles in a copper dish filled to the brim, with a pointed cone on top. He releases a fistful of sand from a definite height to another copper dish—a free-flow. This winnowing confirms beyond doubt that not even a single unwanted and oversized particle is left. Keeping the pitcher with a hole at the bottom on top of a tripod at a precise height, he places the other pitcher on the ground just below the hole. After an accurate measurement, he draws a straight line at a precise distance from the iron stand. Filling the top pitcher to the brim with sand, he holds the tip of a kusha grass erect, plugs the hole with his finger and waits...

The slanting light of the afternoon sun falls on the temple. The tip of the reed casts its shadow on the ground. He removes his finger from the hole of the pitcher as soon as the tip of the shadow touches the line drawn. Thus the sand clock is set on. The sand from the upper pitcher starts flowing like a thin thread. The moment the upper pitcher is emptied, it shall be the exact auspicious moment of *prathama prahara tritiya danda*.

On the lookout for her father, Lilavati enters the temple.

"What's this?" she asks him pointing her finger at the device.

"It's a sand clock".

"Why?"

"To calculate the accurate moment of the marriage. When the upper pitcher completely empties out the sand, we will have to conduct your marriage".

"Yeah, I see," Lilavati says and purses her lip after having a look at the device and the falling sand.

"My darling, don't stay here. Let's go. Never touch the sand clock, or else everything will be spoilt. You had better not enter the temple again today."

The father and the daughter come out of the temple together. While closing the door of the temple, Bhaskaracharya says: "Why have you worn the wedding dress? Go and change it. It will get dirty." Bhaskaracharya then enters the house. He has work lined up for the wedding. The ceremonial handing over of the bride will have to be conducted at the precise moment. Lilavati stands for a while near the door of the temple and then follows her father into the house.

From inside the house, Bhaskaracharya notices that the old man who had accompanied him to Pandit Gagan's house the other day has brought a tender banana plant and kept it near the basil plant. A fuming Bhaskaracharya tries to contain his wrath at the humiliation to be meted out to the girl! He has to be a mute spectator to this mockery of a marriage! What a price the father of a girl has to pay! After the marriage, he will surely ask Pandit Gagan if he has ever prescribed any such remedy for a bridegroom.

Dusk descends soon. Lilavati grows increasingly impatient with time. She waits eagerly for the sand clock to stop. Finally, she dares to dodge her father and enter the temple. Lit with the flame burning in front of the deities, she sees the sand still falling. She leans forward to see the quantity of sand left in the pitcher above. There seems to be plenty of sand still left. She softly closes the door of the temple and returns home, only to follow it up with visits in quick succession. The sand keeps falling in a free-flow. After a long time, the flame inside the temple flickers and goes out. Lilavati finally closes the door and leaves. Clad in the wedding dress, she lies down next to her father. Hugging him, she falls asleep.

The mathematics of a dropped earring

Bhaskaracharya's home has been full of activity since the wee hours. The neighbours of Bhaskaracharya have risen with the lark and raced against the clock to get everything ready. The marriage will be held in the morning. It's a marriage with a difference; the ceremonial handing over of the bride has to be done at the right moment. The father of the groom will arrive after a while. The bridal party is busy offering the guests a warm reception. Lilavati is still in bed when a lady from next door wakes her up.

"Lilavati, it's your wedding. Have you forgotten? Wake up."

"Has the bridegroom come?" Lilavati asks her, her eyes still heavy with sleep.

The woman laughs cheerfully. "He'll come soon. Get up and take a bath or else you will be late," she says.

Lilavati stretches and yawns, only to fall asleep again. The woman then lifts her up in her arms and takes her to the river. After a bath, she is dressed in wedding clothes and ornaments, and taken to the mandapa. On her way back from the *parghat*, she has a glimpse of the bridegroom dressed in a snow-white dhoti-panjabi, with a round turban on the head, sitting near his father. His curly hair is quite visible at the back of his head below the turban. His eyes shine like the inner sides of a water mussel shell. The bride and the groom smile at each other. They find an opportunity to exchange a few words between them.

"What stories do you like—of kings and queens or of demons?" Lilavati asks the young groom.

"Of kings and queens," he replies.

"Can you play hopscotch?"

"No, I can't."

"You can't! Okay then, how many playing pots do you have?"

"Plenty."

"I'll give you my earthen bird."

The bridegroom stares for some moments at his would-be bride. Bhaskaracharya is delighted at seeing the innocent bride and groom lost in a world that is quite different from that of adults. It's time for the ceremonial handing over of his only daughter whom he has brought up carefully and lovingly, playing the role of both parents! His eyes well up with tears. Lilavati is quite oblivious of the fact that she will have to part with her father after the ceremony! Bhaskaracharya has a look at Lilavati again.

"You know, a sand clock is on, inside the temple," says Lilavati to the groom. "My father has done it all. When the sand from the upper pitcher empties into the lower, we shall get married."

The two children run to the temple and take a peep at the sand clock through the slit between the two wings of the door.

The fire for the *homyajna* is lit. It is surrounded by rows of small pitchers. Pandit Gagan starts the rite to ward off the sinister look of an evil planet upon Lilavati.

"Acharya-ji, please be seated. Where is the bride? Let her also sit here," Pandit Gagan says.

Some women then rush to Lilavati to escort her.

"Won't the bridegroom accompany me?"

"No, not now," they reply.

Lilavati is made to sit on a banana leaf near a banana plant standing upright.

"Why have they made me sit here? Won't I sit in the arbour?" She asks her father: "Why here, Father?" Without uttering any word, a helpless Bhaskaracharya simply looks at his daughter.

Pandit Gagan then comes to his rescue, and says: "My dear, you're under the ominous influence of an evil planet. We're performing a rite to dispel it. The actual marriage will be after this rite. But now this banana plant is your bridegroom. Bow down to it and accept it as your husband."

"No, no, no..." she stands up and makes an attempt to rush to her father's arms.

Her effort, however, proves futile as the women press her down and make her sit on the banana leaf. A stunned Lilavati only stares back at her father, who sits unmoved.

"Acharya-ji, what arrangement have you made for the accurate calculation of the right moment?"

"A sand clock is on inside the temple."

"Let's survey the clock. This rite has to be performed before the marriage."

Bhaskaracharya rises, opens the door of the temple and has a look at the clock.

"How is it possible?" He's stunned. "The thread of sand is no longer visible. So fast! How?"

He leans and looks at the clock in disbelief. "Yes, the clock is off." He then inspects the sand in the upper pitcher. It was still not empty!

His clock had never failed him. It was an error-free device. Why did it fail today? The guests and the groom's party are dumbstruck. An error in the calculation of the greatest astronomer, Bhaskaracharya! Impossible and unbelievable! Her father's plight brings tears to Lilavati's eyes.

Bhaskaracharya fails to understand how the hole in the sand clock got blocked. The clock had been functioning perfectly till very late at night. The container had only the finest of sand particles, thoroughly sieved. There's no apparent reason for the hole to get plugged. He dives into the pitcher and starts searching for any unwanted object. After a thorough search, something hard pierces his middle finger and he fishes the object out. It's a *makarkundal*[69]! He had bought it for Lilavati. He comes out from the temple with the earring and stands near the arbour. At a loss for words, he stares at his daughter while his eyes fill with tears. Lilavati quickly stands up, spotting the earring in her father's hands. She realises that the ring on her left ear is missing.

"Take it easy, please. What God wills is for good," Pandit Gagan says, with a comforting hand on Bhaskaracharya's shoulder. "We are mere puppets in the hands of God. What's ordained by fate is inevitable. The calculation of the moment has gone wrong. I hope you will bear with me." Pandit Gagan departs, dumping the girl firmly back on Bhakracharya's lap.

"No marriage now, Father?" the bridegroom asks.

---

69 *Makarkundal:* A heavy piece of earring with the ends shaped like the heads of alligators.

"No, just follow me," Pandit-ji says. Bhaskaracharya looks helplessly at the well-mannered boy. The babbling crowd at the mandapa has vanished. Bhaskaracharya is deserted again. Lilavati stares vacantly at the bridegroom leaving, following the footsteps of his father. The bridegroom too looks back at her.

"Well, time to like you and then leave you," the boy manages to whisper.

Lilavati takes out the other earring, throws it in the fire and flops down on the ground. Crestfallen, she hides face between the knees.

"Enough is enough! I won't take it any more." Bhaskaracharya springs up determinedly, holding his head high and stands upright. He smashes some of the eathen pitchers meant for carrying out the rites of the wedding ceremony into pieces and throws away the banana plant.

"Lilavati, my darling, don't cry over spilt milk. Marriage isn't the ultimate aim in the life of a girl. You may not get married, but you can immortalise your name," Bhaskaracharya consoles his daughter. Lilavati breaks down completely.

"Don't cry, my darling. Dedicate yourself to mathematics. You will have the taste of knowledge. Come on now, I'll teach you mathematics. I'll title the book I'm writing as *Lilavati*. You'll remain immortal. Thousands of children will hold this book close to their heart and study this for generations ahead."

"Will everybody read it?" she asks, peeping through her hands with her head still between her knees. Her crescent eyes twinkle like the new moon.

"Certainly."

She raises her head, has a look at the empty arbour, points her index at the boy going away, and says: "Will the bridegroom deserting me read this book?"

"Without fail."

"Will he keep this book pressed to his heart with love?"

"Certainly."

"Fine. I'm ready, and that's final. Teach me mathematics, Father." Blinking her tears back bravely Lilavati sits in the cross-legged *padmasana* or lotus posture in front of her father and forces a smile. Bhaskaracharya brings his manuscript and begins the first lesson:

"O my dear Lilavati, intelligent and fawn-eyed—a blooming lily is swaying in the breeze between a duck and an egret in a pond. When erect, the lily is half a cubit above the surface of the water and it sinks two cubits under water when swayed by the breeze. Now, work out the depth of the pond, quickly."

Lilavati is engrossed in deep thought and loses herself in the riddle. She is oblivious to the fact that she has already been initiated into the mysteries of mathematics—a world, quite different altogether!

STRAITJACKET

$\mathcal{R}$acing against time...against time. All seemed to be caught in an indecent haste. The last train from the station was about to depart. The ticket checker was in a tearing hurry. He had no time to even toss back a lock of hair out of his eyes. Those in the queue outside his counter too had no time to wait. Those getting tickets were making a dash for the compartments. The jam-packed compartments of the train looked like new matchboxes. The platform was no different. Passengers scrambled from one compartment to another looking for their respective berths. Hordes of people could be seen crowding and jostling around the small tea stalls, book stalls and other shops. Some passengers stood in a queue in front of a room where a woman, clad in a crisp white sari, was serving drinking water. Written distinctly on top of the service-outlet were the words—'Drinking Water / *Peeney ka Pani*'. The station was a sea of humanity. To cap it all; the bursting fumes of exhaust from the engine, the awful screeching of RMS trolleys, trade calls of coolies and hot altercations among passengers on the train had a cumulative deafening effect. A piercing shriek – "Babu *pani*" – let out by a woman hit the eardrums of the passengers at irregular intervals.

*Ghetch ghechang...ghetch ghechang...*went the wheels of the train.

"*Cha garam, cha garam...*" cried the tea seller.

"Babu, pani..."

"Hahahaha! hahaha! ha! *Begum Shahajadi. Ye dunia, ye sansar ek marichika hei*! Haha! hahaha!" The cry for a drop of water from a dying woman got lost in the loud nmonologue of a lunatic—a self-styled nawab.

The nawab, dressed in ragtag clothes, was seated atop a broken wooden packing box—his throne.

It was a moribund woman crying for water at the other end of the platform. Her emaciated body deceived the onlooker's eye, suppressing her gender and the fact that she was a woman! The distinctly visible skeleton was covered by an unwilling skin that had innumerable punctures and gashes all over. Not even an iota of muscle was left. Flies buzzed lazily around the oozing wounds. A leper? It was difficult to ascertain. The seering pain made her take a supine position on the office verandah. The parallel ribs in her chest were quite distinctly visible. The concave abdomen touched her back. Her body, shoulder downwards, lay on the office verandah while the lolling head remained hanging outside. The dishevelled and matted hair was scattered on the platform below. Foamy spittle from the mouth and grime collected in the corners of her eyes mingled with hot tears and dripped to the ground. In the last few moments, her otherwise sunken eyes popped out. She looked at those gathered on the platform and sought a drop of water— 'Pani, babu pani'. The cry, however, failed to echo in the sea of 'civilised' humanity as it blended with the deafening sound of the engine. Hers was a fate same as that of Tantalus. There was drinking water at the tea stall, a woman was busy serving water from a room inside, but there wasn't a single drop to be spared to wet the dying woman's parched lips. Who could give her a drink of water? The tea stall owner or the woman serving water? No, none of them. Why should they? The glass once used by the sick woman would be of no use later. They simply couldn't afford to throw away a glass in the drain.

The death of a begger was nothing unusual for them. And how long could they afford to remain sympathetic towards them? Generosity could spell doom for their business. Conscientious passengers? Often, the labyrinth of laws stood as obstacles. If the dying woman breathed her last after her thirst was quenched, the sympathiser would be in troubled waters. Grilling by policemen, medical examination to ascertain any poisoning, postmortem, witness box ... who would dare to undergo that sort of rigorous harassment? They would rather look the other way till the train departed. Laws, more often than not, warned a sympathiser of the negative consequences of such humane gestures. The law wasn't simply a security shield for people; it was also a tool that clipped their wings. No good Samaritan would dare extend *her* a helping hand. A few well-known personalities from among the passengers lodged a complaint with the station master—raising the issue of the city environment and its pollution. They were thumping the desk. The busy station master telephoned the GRP and the authorities concerned in a hospital. Thus he washed his hands off the responsibility and started puffing a cigarette. As though, it was all a fuss about nothing.

The cry of the beggar, on the other hand, lost its shrill as she was fast losing her lung power. Her mouth was dry. On the verge of death, she didn't want the baton of policemen and medicines from frowning physicians. She only wanted a drop of water.

"*Chai*[70] ..., cold drink, *chai* ...," the trade call of a hawker sounded very close to her.

"*Chai*[71], *chai*. (Yes, I want)". Yes, she wanted the brew but not a cupful or a mugful. Just a drop. The soft drink bottles too

---

70 *Chai*: Brewed tea, pronounced as 'chaye'.
71 *Chai*: "I want", pronounced as 'chayi'.

hoodwinked her by rattling against each other. Rattling? Nay, the bottles were telling her: "You stupid sod! It's not for you. It's for the passengers who have been sweating it out in their long wait for the train to depart."

The mere sight of a drink doesn't quench thirst. There should be somebody to offer her the drink. Thousands of people were near her, but none of them was humane enough to offer her a drop of water. They have straitjackets of all hues to fit into—their jobs, self-interests, the law of the land, aristocracy and the like. The wretched woman looked all around with whatever energy she had left, and closed her eyes again. The lenses in her eyes took the snap of an inverted image of the earth, the most 'developed' of all planets in the solar system. She made an abortive bid to utter a word, but only her lips quivered. No word came out. The station then wore a deserted look. While the train – full to its brim – slowly rolled out of the station, the trouble-torn soul of the woman left her skeletal abode with a jerk, without having its thirst quenched. It was ultimate salvation for the trapped soul which had been impatiently pecking and drumming like a woodpecker at the fragile but straitjacketed frame of her body to find an exit. There was none near the bag of bones; barring two women who had been standing witness to the scene from the very beginning. Nobel laureate for peace, Mother Teresa stood in front, apparently with tearful eyes; at the rear end stood a smiling lady, her right hand raised to shower blessings. This was Indira Gandhi, who had scripted the slogan—*Garibi Hatao*. They too had failed to offer a drop of water to the dying woman. They too were held hostage in their respective straitjackets—Mother Teresa on the hard cover of a book displayed inside a bookshop and Indira Gandhi in the fragments of an old, faded election poster on a wall.

A TALE OF CITIES

*Y*es, it's a tale of cities, not of one or two. Take Mumbai, Chennai, Kolkata, Guwahati...as a case study. It's the same basic storyline. From Google Earth, let's zoom in on any of the cities, say Guwahati...

A sweltering noon. It's the hustle and bustle of city life, with honking cars lined up, nose to tail. The road on the left leads to Fancy Bazar. A billboard stands erect on the right. Rich in carbohydrate, vitamins and minerals–reads the advertisement of a brand of baby food. Followed by the statutory maxim of the World Health Organisation – 'No substitute for breastfeeding' – in almost invisible fine print.

In stark contrast lay a corpse on the footpath! Could be of a mother. A baby breathlessly sucked at the breasts. A begging bowl lay nearby, upside down. The wailing baby stood up and toddled across...a baby boy. A mass of tangled and matted hair on his head.

Coins of mercy fell from pedestrians glued to their mobile phones and commuters in cars and cabs engrossed in surfing the internet—the broad band Wi-Fi. A digital divide! What else could they do? The kid walked over the coins, making a metallic thud and stopped midway. It looked at the other side—a glimmer of hope. The speeding cars screeched to a halt as the child crossed the road and the Omnipresent held its hand. The swamping traffic resumed free flow.

The kid craned his neck to have a better view of a green hoarding. It showed a rhino grazing among the foliage in the Kaziranga National Park, a tourism department's advertisement with a tag line on top—'Incredible India!' Toddling a few steps further, the kid stood in front of another hoarding. A few kids of his age were playing with colourful toys in it. 'Kids' Dreamland', English medium nursery school. A red ball came rolling towards him. The kid on the footpath forgot the ache in his little belly and extended his hands to catch it, but it remained beyond his reach.

The whimpering baby moved ahead, banging against the roadside wall and stopped again. There was an attractive cartoon image on the wall. A boy and a girl were seated on a see-saw—designed like a big pencil painted in colourful stripes! The heading read: 'Let's all go to school'...Sarva Shiksha Abhiyan...a government mission. The kid rushed to catch the pencil—it was a fake one!

The young street urchin limped to another poster—gloomy orphan faces, matted hair. Tears dripping down their cheeks. Known faces? On the backdrop, a tagline—UNICEF HELP. The kid slowly extended his untutored hands.

"Stop it kid. I'm here," another urchin – several years older and in his teens – rushes up to him. He holds the kid's hand. Mobile phone in hand, his is a known face on the streets. A beggar-turned-service provider through his mobile public call office, he offers help to phoneless pedestrians. An innovation, thanks to economist Prof. Mahammad Yunus! The young kid doubles up with shooting pangs of hunger. The teenager leads him on to a pilfered water pipe, offers him a palmful. No, not a substitute. A solace perhaps? His thirst quenched, the kid clings to the older boy, giving a passionate hug in return—an age-old bond of 'eMotion' amidst eBusiness, eLearning and eGovernance advertisement hoardings.

*

Note: *The story is especially dedicated to the famous economist Prof. Mahammad Yunus, Nobel Laureate from Bangladesh, who changed the lives of street children and the poor in South-East Asia.*

THE MUSE OF A MODERN POET

"*C*lad in a *talaphuti*[72], you look like a young zebra lass."

"What do you mean!?" Kalpana asked Amol, while unhooking her earrings in front of the dressing table.

"An African zebra, a jazzy talaphuti-clad Kalpana," sang out Amol in a lilting tone.

That was a perfect hit! Right on the target! Kalpana slumped on the bed in a huff. She felt terribly bored, listening to poetry for three hours at a stretch in the soirée organised by the Tirash group of poets in the town. She didn't feel at ease at the gathering and was not in her elements. To top it all, the simile Amol had just used left her nerves on edge. She hadn't even changed her dress to breathe freely again; there was yet another poem!

The comment rightly reflected the plight which was always in store for the wives of poets. What a simile he had chosen! African zebra! Height of degradation! Kalpana sulked and her blood boiled.

"What has made your blood boil?" Amol fired another salvo.

"Psychoanalysis isn't welcome at the moment!" Kalpana shot back, banging the door behind her and entering the kitchen.

"I asked you because your face is flushed with rage," Amol said, unbuttoning his shirt. "Talaphuti and zebra—wow! What a perfect simile! The theme of a beautiful poem has come to my

---

72 *Talaphuti*: Formal striped lower garment of Bishnupriya Manipuri women.

mind, all of a sudden. It can be a piece for tomorrow's edition of *Tirash*. The editor has requested me many a time for a poem." Amol, chief guest of the gathering of poets, was basking in the self-indulgent glory of his innovative streak of imagination.

A few budding literary talents in town were an enthusiastic bunch. Away from political festoons and fiery slogans demanding justice for people, these budding poets seemed to be the last of the flag-bearers of a true literary movement.

"I've to send the poem tomorrow. These young aspirants get inspired by this small support. It's like giving their morale a boost," Amol muttered to himself.

"Talaphuti...zebra...," he sang out merrily. "If you purse your lips and clam up, who will I talk to? There isn't a third entity in this house yet! The count in the census report is in decimals, just two points..." he continued jestfully.

"Be on the trail of the African zebra. The editor of *Tirash* will be waiting," Kalpana retorted in a sour voice from the kitchen.

"Ha! ha! ha! Psychoanalysis! Telepathy at its best–you live long, at least for me! Plenty of mental communication underway, I can see," Amol replied, laughing.

"Yes, I'm a zebra, a beast."

"Hey, what do you mean?"

Amol entered the kitchen and tried explaining. "What I mean is..."

"The fact is that you take a macho pride in degrading women. Though you project yourself as modern, you're yet to rid yourself of male chauvinism," Kalpana brusquely cut him short.

"Is this the sum total, including the compound interest, of the evaluation of your husband's character since our marriage?" Amol asked.

"Perhaps you're joking, but what I said is the stark truth—this is how men rate women," she retorted.

"I made the remark in jest, but you have taken it otherwise. See, a woman is the true portraiture of nature—a combination of creation, destruction, affection, cruelty, desire, worship and the like; all elements beautifully blended in one. It's the woman who gives birth to the man. Which is why, she's the muse of all poets, regardless of sex..."

"That's enough! The lectures and recitations at the poets' meet are still to be digested. Compound interests! You could have earned extra bucks through tuition had you studied mathematics, instead of literature," she took a dig at him, and moved to the dining table to serve dinner. She had cooked a meal before going out.

*

They had their meal. Amol made an attempt to coax a piqued Kalpana, trying to make her feel at ease, but to no avail. Her laconic replies of "umm", "oh", and the like, devoid of any frills, let Amol know that she was still simmering under a spell of bad mood. Finally, having finished all her chores, she retired to bed. Amol smiled at her but she didn't reciprocate.

"If Monalisa threw such a sullen glare at Leonardo, what would he..."

She took the long pillow and placed it in the middle of the bed, parallel to her, to drive a wedge between them. Finally she turned her back to him and made an attempt to fall asleep. It was enough of a hint for Amol that his remark of 'zebra' wasn't taken well and remained as a sore prick. Scratching his head, he made an attempt to divert the underlying meaning of her gesture, "It's okay. I won't write anything about long pillows anymore, but just listen to me."

Kalpana shut off one of her ears with her arm, while the other was pressed against the pillow. Thus, she wouldn't hear a word that Amol would probably tell her.

"What should I do?" Amol scratched his head again, and murmured to himself. He was in a fix—should he write the poem or coax Kalpana. He knew it would take hours to coax a sulking Kalpana and bring her back to normal. On the other hand, if he missed the very mood to write the poem, it would never come to him again. In the morning, he had to race against the clock to reach office. He held an office job as literature didn't help sustain a living; instead it burnt a big hole in the pocket. He glanced once at Kalpana, and then at the table. A white paper on the lamplit table was waiting for him like a patient lying prostrate in an operation theatre.

"Let me write," Amol murmured under his breath, leaving the bed. He stole a glance at Kalpana, twisted the tip of his tongue, and murmured under his breath, his voice laced with an evil leer–"Sweet sleep, come here; here lies my dear!" He then gave a raunchy peck on her eyelids and made a quick escape.

∗

Kalpana literally buried her face in the pillow. She had no choice but to sulk and pass another sleepless night. A hectic schedule awaited her next morning. Writers, by nature, were insomniacs. In the past four years, she had to pass many a sleepless night. One night, while she was yawning sleepily, Amol demanded her attention. "Just listen to this line," he called out excitely. "Does it sound fine?" Another night, when a drowsy, nodding Kalpana found even sitting upright a task, Amol requested earnestly, "Just read out this poem loudly dear! "Let's see how it sounds? Oh wait, I need to bring in some changes in the metaphor." On yet another occasion, in the middle of the night, when she had risen to visit the washroom, her eyes heavy with sleep, Amol had quickly picked that moment to share his views on poetry. "Since you have woken up just listen to the theme of this poem," he requested. "Feeling sleepy, are you? Come on, you sleep every night! Kamalesh has written a critique of this poem. This is the write-up. Now, the next theme..."

*

She hadn't kept an account of her sleepless nights—of all the laughing, crying, sulking and sitting...till dawn. Not getting enough sleep, she remained stressed out through the day. What did Amol say while cajoling her? She wracked her brains, trying to remember.

"Oh! I won't write anything about long pillows and bolsters," he had promised. Kalpana pressed her mouth against the pillow just to stifle her laughter while her body shook silently.

*

She couldn't sleep the night that Amol finally wrote the poem. And sleep eluded her when it was published.

"Eureka, eureka, I got it," Amol exclaimed loudly, breaking the silence of the night. Kalpana woke up with a jolt; it sent shock waves down her.

"What! What is it?" she blurted out instinctively.

"A pair of soft long pillows, creamy bolsters!" Amol replied.

"Long pillows!" Kalpana exclaimed in astonishment. She pinched Amol just to ascertain whether he was talking in his sleep. Amol rose from the bed, rushed to the table and heaved a sigh of relief after writing a few lines hurriedly. Did she have any chance to fall asleep again?

Not with the discussion coming up next on the problems faced by poets not using the right similes to describe women's thighs and the diatribes they faced for the inappropriate use of similes. While some were greeted with derision for using the 'cold' imagery of banana trunks, others faced adverse criticism for the 'hardness' in the use of the imagery of a pair of ivory-white elephant tusks. Anyway, these were all clichés. An elated Amol basked in the pleasure of having innovated an appropriate simile for a woman's thighs. Kalpana, on the other hand, was robbed of all sleep that night.

Finally when the poem was published, a blushing Kalpana hung her head in utter embarrassment. The last few lines of the poem read:

>...Afflicted with physical agony
>I hung my head down.
>The pair of creamy long bolsters—
>The two warm thighs of Kalpana,
>Offered me a peaceful abode.

"Oh how disgusting this reads! What have you written? Why have you dragged me in? We're yet to complete two years of married life!" Kalpana protested vehemently, blushing like a beetroot in embarrassment.

"The Kalpana in this poem isn't you. This is the muse, the poet's imagination," explained Amol.

"Even then, how can you use such explicit terms and imagery?"

"Muse Erato is like Urvashi, or Venus...What role has artificial clothing to play in poetic inspiration?"

"It's just you who thinks so! Oh dear! What will my elder brothers and parents think after reading this?"

Kalpana went scarlet with embarrassment and wept silently through the night. Her mind seamlessly played out the earlier unsavoury events, once again giving her a restless night!

The memories of that night are out to spoil my sleep tonight too, she thought to herself, between her sobs. No, I won't let that happen. I've to find a way out. Let him spend the night with his muse the 'zebra', not me.

She too would write—a letter to her sister advising her to keep a safe distance from litterateurs, and not to marry any of them. Or else, she too would meet the same fate. Pulling a light cotton sheet over her body, Kalpana made an abortive effort to fall asleep. Her mind wandered down memory lane to their wedding night and their bridal bed. That night too was...

Next morning, Amol transformed into the full-fledged bank professional – officer 'Sinha' – his regular corporate image. Racing against time – doing the routine rounds of the bathroom, dressing room and breakfast table in lightning speed – he managed to reach office in time. In all his hurry however, he didn't forget to carry the poem he had written the previous night. Kalpana didn't feel like asking him about it.

Let him write whatever he wished. She was quite done with it. When her earrings dangled, he imagined a pendulum in the motion. And when she wore a talaphuti, he created a female zebra in her guise!

*

Ting-tong, ting-tong! A few days later the calling bell rang around half past four in the evening. A beaming Kalpana, waiting all day for the welcome jingle, quickly opened the door to find a tired-looking Amol outside. He joined Kalpana at the dining table after a quick shower, silently trying to gauge her mood. Kalpana had noticed the magazine lying folded on the bedside table on her way to the dining table.

Take a look at it? Leave it, let it be. What's the use? What has he written? Fine, let me read it, once. He won't know.

Kalpana was in a dilemma. Stealing a glance towards the dining room, she picked up the magazine and opened it. Oh! The poem had been published! She ran her eyes down the page.

Zebra
Amol Sinha

Africa, dense, erotic, green;
Illuminated by a young zebra lass
striking up a staccato beat,
pitted against the rough edge of passion.
Painted like the black and ivory keys of a harmonium—
she is the symphony of life.
Only she can create and blend the seven colours of the earth;
Be as dewy as the dawn and burn bright as the flaming white lily.
Only she can make a heart throb.
A zebra lass of Africa lies snug in my arms;
Her eyes melting in the dream of a fresh life.
The talaphuti-clad lass is in her periodic cycle,
Of creation and motherhood.
A rose blooms at night
From the hues of blood.

With the magazine in her hand, she cut short to the dining table and snapped at Amol.

"Can't you leave me out and write this stuff...what you call poems? Why do you keep dragging me into your writing?" She fumed at him, her words coming in one breath.

"Oh, but have I?"

"What do these concluding lines signify?"

"How can you say that's you? What proof do you have?"

"Barring me, who else could be in your tight hug? Or is there actually someone from your office?"

"Come on. The 'I', 'my' mentioned in the poem isn't just Amol! It can be any man. Understood? *Te chal...*"

"Don't you feel embarrassed while writing all this stuff? Speak up and speak the truth!"

Amol continued to eat without caring to reply.

"I can't believe that you could stoop so low. Couldn't you have a male zebra in the poem instead?" Kalpana hurled another question at her husband.

"Ha! ha! ha! Quite evidently you had geography as a subject in college. You must place the zebras of Africa against the backdrop of literature – not geography necessarily – to get your answer", Amol quipped, rising and walking to the wash basin.

*

It was Sunday. Kalpana and Amol's drawing room wore a warm look. Two journalists from Guwahati had come to interview Amol the poet to get a glimpse of his life and home. Kalpana was busy playing the perfect hostess. She basked in the reflected glory of her husband who possessed that special elusive charm – the *je ne sais quoi* – which set him apart from the rest of his fold. After a long discussion involving literature and academics with Amol, the two scribes began quizzing Kalpana on her husband's personal life. The conversation rolled on pleasantly, the day being a holiday. What did Amol like to write about? What was he fond of? Finally, one of them asked her, "How do you personally rate Amol's poetry? Do you like them?"

On the pretext of scrubbing his face with a handkerchief, Amol covered his mouth and waited for Kalpana's response.

Kalpana shot Amol a sideways glance, and replied with a cheeky smile: "If I rate his poems as good, the adjective 'good' may, I think, lose its elegance and class to an extent."

A stunned Amol craved to praise his wife's verbal dexterity. A most befitting reply had come from his muse! She had acquired much from him, Amol realised.

"It seems that a poet of repute being your better half, you're a contented lady yourself. Isn't that so?" asked the other journalist.

"If that wasn't true, the tea you just had wouldn't have the right proportion of sugar," she replied, sending everyone into peals of laughter.

"Now, before we leave, may we click a joint photograph of the two of you...preferably lifesize?" An earnest request from the visitors, and a most natural one landed soon after.

"Yeah, sure! Please wait a moment." Kalpana went into her bedroom and Amol followed. Kalpana was swiftly changing into a talaphuti and an *inafi*[73], standing in front of her dressing table, staring into the mirror. Spotting Amol in the mirror she asked, "Won't you dress up?"

"I need to go shopping," Amol said.

"Shopping right now! Why?" A stunned Kalpana asked him.

"To buy a striped *lungi*," he said.

"A lungi?" she asked.

"Yes, to match your talaphuti. I will be a male zebra, or else you'll accuse me of degrading you. You would be in a huff again," he said.

Kalpana laughed aloud, pulled out a dhoti from the cupboard and handed it to Amol.

"Put this on. Actually I don't get angry with you."

---

73 *Inafi*: A traditional Bishnupriya Manipuri shawl for women.

"Oh, don't you? Then why do you keep firing bullets of accusation at me these days?" Amol blurted out, draping the dhoti around his waist.

Kalpana stared at him and finally replied, "Poets need to be reminded with such occasional bullets from their partners that they have wives who too, aren't devoid of desires."

"W...h...a...t..!" Amol gasped in surprise, recalling the kiss that he had planted on Kalpana's eyelids the other night, breaking out in full-throated laughter. With a happy smile, the duo posed as a loving couple in front of the camera.

*

Note: *The story is exclusively dedicated to the spouses of poets and writers.*

THE THIRST OF MANDILA

*K*undalei basks in the sunny winter afternoon of the month of Maagh[74]. She combs the ends of the tuft of hair carefully with a brush after a prolonged oil massage. The tuft of hair tied in a ponytail dazzles in the sunlight. Mandila, her six-year-old granddaughter has her eyes fixed on the ponytail—her body resting on an arched arm of her grandmother and her tired head lolling against her shoulder. She keeps staring at the ponytail, despite the tiredness. Her beaming eyes are forever immersed in dreams. The eyes are dreamy—lovely! The fawn-eyed girl keeps looking at the tuft while it is massaged with oil and lovingly brushed. It's a new development in her, not more than three months old.

"Mandila," Granny calls her.

"Hoon," she responds.

"How long will you keep looking at the ponytail? It's your mom's, ill-fated!"

"Where's my mom?" Mandila asks her.

"She's up there," Kundalei says, raising her hand along with the brush, her eyes set heavenward.

"From there she's watching my plight! Leaving me behind to suffer lifelong like rice husk endlessly steaming in the dying embers. She's playing a trick. My darling, I've been singed. My

---

74 Maagh: The Indian calendar month stretching from the middle of January to the middle of February.

days are also numbered. I'm joining you soon. Butter pilferer, naughty Nandalal![75] Why don't you call me early?"

As and when Mandila asks her grandmother about her mother, the old woman points her index skywards, talks incoherently and sobs her heart out through plaintive songs. Mandila too, often loses herself in the sky and does the same today. The azure sky! Mandila's eyes reflect the blue.... She imagines a big village in the sky. Lamps are lit in lines every evening. Mandila actually witnesses all these visions. Her mother lives in that village. Yes, she's there. Mandila believes it wholeheartedly. The only missing link is: everybody else has hair on the head but her mother's hair is with her Granny—a disembodied ponytail. A thoroughly confused Mandila has a glance at her Granny. By then Kundalei has completed a song and is brushing the tuft of hair again. Her eyes brimming with tears, she chants, "My darling will wear this when she grows up. Her mother has left it behind for her."

"Grandma, when will I grow up?"

"Girls grow up like arum plants, honey. Today's kid is a youthful girl tomorrow, all at once."

Mandila's eyes flash. She smiles. Kundalei heaves a deep sigh. Had she been alive to see her daughter's D-Day! As though to extend the span of her life up to the wedding of her grand-daughter, Kundalei gives a long brush stroke to the ponytailed hair from its base to the tip, and rises. She spreads out the ponytail on a heap of paddy sheaths laid out in the courtyard. Her daughter-in-law Madhabi had a glowing golden complexion resembling ripe paddy. The tall pile of paddy with the hair spread across it looks like her daughter-

---

75 Butter pilferer naughty Nandalal: Reference to child Krishna who was extremely fond of homemade butter and mischievously stole butter from the homes of *gopinis*—the milkmaids.

in-law seated for hairdressing. In this pose, as often as not, she had untangled and braided her hair. She was meticulous in her hairdo.

"My darling!" sighs Kundalei.

"*Ine*[76], cut my hair and keep it for Mandila. Give it to her when she grows up. Why are you crying?"

Madhabi's dying wishes, uttered barely five days before her death, still resonate in Kundalei's ears. Kabiraj Rupa had given up all hope. Madhabi lay in the shadow of death; it was evident in her falling pulse rate. Well aware of that, Madhabi asked her mother-in-law to cut her hair.

Everything remains vivid in Kundalei's memory. Cutting Madhabi's luxuriant growth of hair while she lovingly pats her toddler daughter, Mandila. Tears stream down her cheeks, drenching the pillow. She had nourished these tresses all her life—now to be left behind at her hour of death as the last parting gift for her only baby daughter. While innocent Mandila smiles, her mother weeps. Madhabi and Modana had been blessed with Mandila, several years after their marriage. She was their first child and Madhabi's last too.

*

"Mandila, bow down. The wick has gone out," Kundalei tells her granddaughter. She's performing the fortune-fetching rite with the little girl while the sun goes down at the horizon where the paddy field ends. Today they have completed harvesting. There is no sheath of paddy to be seen in the field. Kundalei is here to take home the last sheath of the season. A small space

76 *Ine*: Salutation to mother-in-law.

– cleared of straw and plastered with clay and cow dung – has some fruits, betel-nuts, a wick and a brass pot of water. Children grazing cattle and gleaning dry cow dung cakes and grains left behind by reapers have flocked there for the fruits on offer. All of them bow down when Kundalei asks them to do so. Kundalei gives them *folal.*[77] What remains is carrying Fortune – Goddess Lakshmi – home.

"Beware! While taking fortune home, the holder of the paddy sheath can't utter a single word. You know, wealth has wings. Fortune flies away as and when its fetcher opens her mouth," Kundalei cautions Mandila.

The sheath of paddy is placed on top of a brass pot filled with clear water. Mandila takes the pot, places it on top of an *irufi*[78] curled into a roll of buffer and balances both on her head. Clad in an *angaluri*[79]improvised from a snow-white irufi, she's a perfect lookalike of a young Madhabi. Her look comes as a shock for her grandma. Had Madhabi been alive, she would have performed this rite. Leading from the front with the Fortune is Mandila, with Kundalei at her heels. Raising her hands up, Kundalei weeps: "Madhabi, look at your daughter. She's taking Fortune home. She has succeeded you."

Mandila, however is in her own world. She has her eyes set on small ridged plots of land. Her shadow that has been cast on the straw-covered ground lengthens with the approach of sunset. Her long shadow produces much mirth in her. She's grown up, all of a sudden! She's about to tell her grandmother of this, but stops short abruptly—wealth has wings! She presses her lips tightly

---

77 *Folal:* Fruit meal prepared by mashing banana, flattened rice (*chewra*), parsed paddy etc. together and mixing it with milk.

78 *Irufi:* A Bishnupriya Manipuri towel.

79 *Angaluri:* A lower garment for Bishnupriya Manipuri women.

against each other and keeps walking with a smile, looking at her long shadow. She enters home with Fortune, her grandmother with old and sad memories.

*

"Ima, see, I've grown up," Mandila tells her aunt, soon after entering home. She also shows a hem of the irufi she's clad in.

"Oh, I see," Rebati says.

The child calls Rebati 'Ima', mother. What else should she call a woman who has cradled and lovingly raised her? She's a newly-wedded bride for others, but only 'Ima' for Mandila. When her Granny points her index towards the sky to show the whereabouts of her mom, though she senses a certain mismatch in the two, Mandila has never had any doubt about her 'mother'. Of late, for about the last three months, she has been casting a doubt over Rebati's motherhood, particularly after Rebati gave birth to a baby. The lap of Mandila's Ima has been taken over and possessed by the newborn. The new baby has robbed Mandila of her mother. While informing Rebati of her sudden growth, Mandila noticed the baby suckling noisily at her Ima's breast—chuk, chuk, chuk...

Mandila feels thirsty whenever she hears breastfed babies clucking at their mothers' breast. She inches towards Rebati slowly, and sits—her tiny body resting on an arched hand and the head lolling against the shoulder. Rebati often pulled Mandila to her lap, but never breastfed her, not even now. "She had kept the milk hidden in her bosom for the newborn, depriving me. For shame!" Mandila sulks, and wanders off in a huff. The continued clucking of the baby and the ambience of the room redolent with the musty-sweet smell of breastmilk make her thirst grow insatiable. She feels her mouth drying up right down to the stomach. She craves for the taste of mother's milk, swallows saliva repeatedly to quench her thirst, but to no avail. The insatiable thirst makes her stand up and hug Rebati from behind. She cajoles her by rubbing her face in Rebati's hair. She keeps kissing Rebati on her cheeks once, twice, thrice...but her insatiable thirst goes unattended.

"Stop it! You've choked me. The baby will suffer from reflex coughing," Rebati says and frees herself from Mandila's tight hug. The mere act ruffles up the sulking mind of Mandila. Rebati is oblivious of the emotions she has stirred up in the little girl.

"She doesn't allow me to kiss her. Always preoccupied...baby, baby, baby..." Mandila steps off in a huff once again. Taking two steps back, she stands still with her arms locked over her chest.

*

The baby has dozed off while suckling. Rebati lulls her baby to a deeper sleep, gently lowers it in the low-floor cot and leaves the room. She fails to notice Mandila sulking behind her back. Staring at the baby for a long while, for some unknown reason Mandila inches towards it. She feels happy watching the chubby, innocent face of the sleeping infant. The soft mouth, the sweet smell of breast milk, the two red lips and a drop of milk on the upper lip of the baby allure her. Slowly she bends down and softly touches the lips of the newborn with her own, only to make the baby apprehensive and cry aloud. A shocked Mandila steps back. Frustrated and enraged, she scratches the baby on its tender nose.

"You're hurt? You deserve it!" she says, scowling. The baby screams loudly.

"Oh what happened? What have you done?" Rebati rushes in and picks up the baby in her arms. "Oh, why have you scratched the baby?" she exclaims upon noticing the faint scratch.

Unable to find a proper response, Mandila only replies with a soft "Hoon, hoon."

"Why don't you go and play in the courtyard?" Rebati does not sound angry, nor does she scold Mandila. Yet Mandila's lips start quivering and her eyes brim with tears. Rubbing her eyes hard to wipe them away, she goes out to complain to her granny.

*

But where's her grandmother? After fetching fortune from the fields, she has gone somewhere, perhaps, to the priest's house. Whom to complain to? Yet, the complaint has to be lodged. She could certainly complain to her father. But what exactly was the complaint? "She scolds me, doesn't breastfeed me. She isn't my Ima. She is just the baby's mom." Rubbing her eyes, Mandila waits eagerly for her father to come home. But he doesn't come. He is a peripatetic father! Where does he go every day? How long could she keep staring at the gate? She starts looking at the situation from other angles as well. The tuft of hair from her mother spread out over a sheath of paddy catches her eye. She climbs up the heaped paddy and brings the hair down. Mom's hair!

She rubs the tips of the hair over her chubby cheeks—they prickle against her soft skin, just as when her father kisses her with his bristling moustache.

"Hee...hee...," she giggles. Now she presses the middle of the ponytail against her cheeks. It's smooth. She buries her face in it. A smell, same as the one she gets in the hair of her aunt, hits her senses. It's mom's smell! She buries her face in the hair repeatedly and soaks in the lovely smell. She imagines her mother staying in a skyhigh nest of sorts, of the kind that eagles and hawks build on treetops or cliff edges. Finally having been able to reach her mother staying so high up, Mandila is overjoyed and drowns herself in caressing and cajoling her. She suddenly ends up kissing her mother's cheeks. But where are the cheeks? Where's the face? She has only the tuft of hair of her mother in her hands. What did the face of her mother look like? Seeking replies to all such queries, Mandila stares at the sky. Her beaming eyes are dreamy—wonderful!

✳

Each and every treetop nest in the celestial village of Mandila's mother is lit brightly with a lamp. Her home on the earth lights lamps too. Yes, it is evening. A canopy of fog descends and wraps the earth all around. Theirs is a two-shed thatched house. Huddled around the portable hearth set in a broken cauldron in the verandah are Kundalei, Mandila's father Modana and two of his friends. All of them have tightly wrapped their shawls around their heads as scarves. Had they sat inside the house, Rebati would have hesitated to move freely in front of her elder brother-in-law. The house and the verandah are filled with the wafting aroma of the savoury *yannam*[80] cooking in the kitchen. The house is dark as Rebati has taken the lamp to the kitchen. The fire in the verandah illuminates the house to an extent. Lighting a *bidi* from the fire in the hearth, one of Modana's friends remarks: "Don't be such a fool, Modana. It's fate! Had it been a son, there would have been every reason for a second thought. For one who will soon leave for the home of others..."

"Let the dead past bury its dead. The family needs an extra pair of female hands. Aunt suffers from fragile health. The only daughter-in-law at home can neither do household chores nor

---

80 *Yannam:* A spicy aromatic plant.

can she work at the paddy field with a suckling baby," says the other friend.

"Yes, my dear. Ours is a family of farmers. Do we have time to waste for the one who is no longer alive? I do cry for her, everyday. What else can we do? Oh, *obujh mon ti...* (Oh, the restless mind)." Kundalei has a harrowing time herself, unable to accept the death of Madhabi, and in a bid to pacify her son and make him agree to a second marriage, ends up singing a soulful song. Modana maintains a stony silence leaning against the wall while listening to all the advice. The veins in his hands stand out distinctly, overworked with the load he has to shoulder during this harvesting season. His chin has a dark stubble of a week's growth. He looks worried and problem-ridden with little Mandila to look after as well as manage the harvest season. He has in mind the plight of his younger brother working in the army. Newly married, he can't take his wife to his place of posting. After every earned leave, he leaves home alone, for the sake of the family. A family just doesn't get along and manage home and hearth without a capable woman. This apart, Modana is yet to reconcile to the death of Madhabi, and feels as though she's still alive. He feels her presence around him, while sowing and harvesting paddy in the field.

"The girl is polite and well-mannered, quite an expert in household chores—she has plenty of attributes. Don't say 'no.' Mandila too will get a mother's care and affection," one of the friends says.

"Don't ponder over the consequences. All step mothers aren't alike. You should go and see the girl tomorrow. If you give your nod, next Falgun would be an ideal time for the wedding."

Modana tries to lay his finger on a strong enough reason for opting to go in for his second marriage. Madhabi had told him once—"Masculine love! They don't even let a year elapse to wed another, if there is a bereavement. They hop between loved ones. And the friendly advices come for free. 'The family needs a woman, so on, and so forth...for them such pretences keep the family going. We, on the other hand, have no way out but to live a dull monochromatic life, playing second fiddle to the male worshippers at any ritual."

"I'm a man with a difference" Modana had claimed. "Check me out if the occasion arises." The litmus test is today. How should he explain to Madhabi's soul when he confronts it, as to why he has to marry again? For himself? Impossible! For a scion? Doesn't he think Mandila as his own? His sister-in-law is overburdened with all the household chores. Will Madhabi's soul buy the argument? For Mandila? Judicious enough! He seems to have found a foothold. The kid will get her mother back. If she gets affection at this tender age, she may...

"Fate rules everywhere. Will she ever come back?" Kundalei advises him to come to terms with the reality. What they say fall on the deaf ears of Modana; and when the talk centres on the death of Madhabi, someone raises a quiet protest from within the house. Modana hears it distinctly. Is it an illusion? He looks at the others sitting near him, and then scans inside the house. The house seems to have grown darker. The faint light coming from the kitchen is a poor substitute to bright lamps and dimly illuminates parts of the house, throwing dark shadows at corners. He looks at his old bedroom—a storehouse of memories. Inside, it bears the memory of Madhabi.... Oh, who's there! Modana stands still. Who's there leaning by the wall of his wife's chamber? He enters the chamber. It's little Mandila, a perfect lookalike of Madhabi. Modana hugs and kisses her lovingly.

"Monigo, what is the matter?" he asks her.

"Hoon, mom is there," she replies.

"Yes, she's here. You're a perfect reflection of your mother."

"No, she's really here," Mandila keeps on insisting.

"Where's she?" asks Modana.

"There." Mandila points her finger skywards. Modana heaves a deep sigh of sorrow. He notices that everybody in the house is looking at him and his daughter.

His sisterer-in-law, Rebati also stands near the door of the kitchen holding the lamp. The disbelief in her father makes Mandila hold Modana's forefinger and pull him along. Modana stops her with the apprehension that he'll be led to his sister-in-law. But she keeps pulling her father to another direction. A stunned Modana surrenders and follows her. Mandila lifts the mattress of her grandmother's bed, scoops out the tuft of carefully oiled and brushed hair belonging to her mother and swiftly hands it over to her father, raising goosebumps in Modana's body. He has his hands full of Madhabi's hair, still fresh and oily. His hands start shivering and his eyes well up with hot tears. Others in the house, too, have moist eyes. An innocent Mandila simply stares at her father and clutches on to his knees.

❄

Rebati admires Mandila's elegance, sometimes dressing her in bridal finery and often in the attire of a young mother. Mandila loves imitating Rebati. If Rebati is a bride, Mandila will be so; if Rebati is a mother, Mandila too, will be one. Copying Rebati is a game—her pleasure and passion.

"Monigo, don't scratch the baby," Rebati reminds her.

"Hoon," she responds to her aunt, promising not to.

"Play near the baby with the doll." Giving Mandila the doll, Rebati leaves the room. The shadows lengthen and evening descends. Soon a canopy of fog envelopes the surroundings. Kundalei has gone to the nearby hamlet to help with the arrangements of a *shraddha*[81]. Under peer pressure, Modana has also gone to see the girl—the prospective bride they had talked about the previous night. Wrapping her head with a scarf, Rebati leaves for the paddy-thrashing ground with a shovel in hand. She has to shovel and collect the thrashed paddy into a heap before it is too dark. She prays silently but fervently, "Oh God! Don't let this proposal go out of hand. I'm fed up."

Mandila, alone at home, meanwhile transforms into a mother. "Sweetheart...my goody-goody honey," she mutters, hugging the doll with great affection, asserting her motherhood. She flops down on the floor. Putting the doll under her *inafi* and holding it with the other hand she starts breastfeeding it. Unveiling the head, she's untangling the hair just as her aunt does. She, however, feels something incomplete. Her hair is too short. How long will she untangle hair in the air? A useless exercise! All of a sudden, she remembers her mother's tuft of hair. Rushing to her grandmother's bed, she takes the ponytailed hair and wears it. She then enters Rebati's bedroom and looks at herself in a small looking glass. Her hair tumbles down in a dark cascade down her back. She giggles and so does the little mom in the looking glass. She tries untangling the hair—her hair doesn't end till it reaches down to the knees. She giggles again and claps in delight. How strange! Now she doesn't want to breastfeed the doll anymore. She fixes her eyes on the newborn sleeping in his cot.

"Up you come." She lifts the baby gently and swaddles it. The baby puckers its face. Mandila is prompt enough to softly whisper in its ears, "I won't scratch you. I won't anymore."

Maybe, an understanding is reached, and the baby sleeps on. Mandila sits near the bamboo wall and puts the baby to her chest.

---

81 *Shraddha*: Last rites.

While she untangles her hair, the baby starts looking for warm breasts in her flat chest, taking her to be Rebati. With the baby's tender lips fondling her flat chest, a chain of ripples spreads across her entire being and makes her body sway like tufts of ripe paddy in a mild breeze. She had long been craving for such warmth from the bosom of Rebati. Today, imitating a nursing mother and enjoying an entirely new emotion by herself the little girl laughs and sings blissfully. She discovers that her parched tongue is moist, and it tastes sweet too.

IN SEARCH OF AN IMMORTALISING HERB

*S*hankhaleima stood at the crossroads of three pathways at Jirania.

It was dusk. With Shankhaleima stood seven-year-old Babashou, smiling at a cow's hoof marks on the ground. Standing with her hands pressed against her waist, Babashou's grandmother, Shankhaleima tried reining him back: "Give a broad grin, show your teeth and appeal to the Tooth Fairy.... You should say, "Bobei, oh Bobei, give me your fine teeth." While speaking to her grandson, she looked up skywards and made a fervent appeal to Bobei for a trouble-free teething of her young grandson.

A group of children, all friends of Babashou, enjoyed the street play, grinning and chuckling at the show. A shy Babashou too, tried to laugh like his friends. He hung his head down because he was praying to Bobei for his tooth, and that too, in full public glare.

"Why are you smiling with your teeth clenched? Have you abandoned all thoughts of the Tooth Fairy!" Shankhaleima chided her grandson.

A sprightly eighty-year-old, Shankhaleima was the oldest woman in Jirania village. Her complexion had turned slightly yellowish with age but her back was ramrod staright and she did not use a walking stick. Her elongated earlobes spoke of the heavy earrings she had worn in her youth. With age, those earrings had been replaced with two ginger lilies. The countless

wrinkles on her face were an eloquent testimony of her expertise
and local knowledge—she was a living example of ethnic life
and the best source of traditional knowledge.

Shankhaleima was the only dependable occultist at Jirania.
Appeasing ghosts, calling the departed souls of ancestors
prior to any rituals, warding off evil spirits, giving offerings
to appease Pahangpa, finding remedies for the problems
faced by lactating mothers were some of the popular areas
where she used her expertise. There was none in the village
fit to receive this traditional knowledge from her and retain it
for the generations to come. Only her daughter had learnt a
few of the chants and tricks. The number of believers of the
supernatural forces was on the decline. Her son, Kartiksena
for example had scant regard for the occult. Kartiksena was
a changed man after his marriage. Shankhaleima could have
disciplined her daughter-in-law had Kartiksena done as she
had advised him. She blamed it all on the school teacher
Madanchand who had dealt a severe blow to her practice of
the occult by brainwashing her son and daughter-in-law as
well as the other villagers. Despite that, Shankhaleima kept
alive all the charms and incantations she had received from
her gurus. She did not have too many years to live; the old
practice would die out completely with her death.

With a solemn bow to Bobei, she massaged her hair with
her palms. Her cropped hair flew like a white flag, free from
any bondage of illusion or sensuality, waiting to get burnt in the
bonfire on the occasion of the birth of Sri Chaitanya Deva.

＊

Dressed in denim trousers and a khadi kurta with its sleeves
rolled up, Madanchand reached the very spot and alighted from

his bicycle. His brown face had a stubble of a few days. He was the tutor of Babashou and Imashou. Without a government job after clearing his B.Sc. examination, he gave private tuitions and met his ends fairly well, having gradually crossed the age-bar of government jobs while on the hunt for jobs. He had tied the knot with Shefalika of the adjoining hamlet. Madanchand smiled at the sight of Babashou grinning with his teeth out over the footprint of a cow, following the age-old custom.

"Grand-aunt, what are you doing?" Madanchand asked Shankhaleima. Spotting his teacher, Babashou stood up and hid himself behind his grandmother. He covered the gap of his upper incisors given to the tooth fairy, with his upper lip. Other boys standing around left quickly.

"You know, Babashou has a teething problem. I'm praying to Bobei for an easy teething," Shankhaleima replied.

"Oh, grand-aunt, how many teeth does Bobei have? More than thirty-two?" Madanchand questioned the grand old woman much to her annoyance. She asked him back: "Why?"

"Poor Bobei might live his life without a single tooth, as all the parents of the village keep praying for their children's fine teeth in exchange of the milk teeth," the teacher said, taking a dig at the occultist.

"You are talking rubbish again," an annoyed Shankhaleima said.

"It would have been better to smile over the footprint of a preceptor instead of that of a cow. I'm afraid lest Babashou get the teeth of a cow and starts to ruminate," the teacher said. The old woman hurled another set of angry words and abuses at Madanchand. It was enough for Babashou to flee the scene.

"Quiet, I say! You were in the jaws of death, struck by a rigorous bout of loose motions," she thundered. "It was I who saved you by appeasing the evil spirit, offering an oblation at this crossroads. You're a tall and stout man today; I had applied

special powers to transmit your infectious disease to a fish."
Shankhaleima muttered angrily to herself on her way back
home. The pair of dangling ginger lilies in her earlobes and her
loose flabby arms danced with the motion of her angry strides.
Madanchand smiled at her and rode away on his bicycle.

*

After evening prayers, Shankhaleima sat talking to Taraleima, her
only daughter married in the same village. Her daughter-in-law,
Gouri, a pretty young mother of two kids, served them tea in
brass bowls. Sipping the brew, Shankhaleima showered praise
on her. "Your sister-in-law is matchless in making tea," she told
her daughter. Our tea has a distinct flavour. Drinking tea at other
homes? It's nauseating! Yuck!" Shankhaleima grimaced. Gouri
simply smiled at Taraleima and walked away silently. She knew
that Shankhaleima would keep showering praises on her till the
last drop of the brew and then turn into a complaining mother-in-
law. Gouri was immune to her abusive mother-in-law and turned
a deaf ear to her complaints. In reality, Shankhaleima bore her
no ill-will.

Shankhaleima pushed the emptied brass bowl aside.
Taraleima filled a hookah and served it to her mother in a hubble-
bubble made of a Kanchanpuri coconut shell.

Taraleima liked to spend most of her leisure hours with her
mother, trying her best to inherit her knowledge. Why should
her mother's treasure trove of knowledge go waste? Who else
was there to inherit? Her brother was under the iron grip of his
spouse. He too had scant regard for anything supernatural.

"Mother, Monigo is prone to nightmares. He says his late
grandfather stares at him with eyes wide open from the bamboo
grove," Taraleima said.

"The *tithi* for paying oblation to forefathers is approaching. You know, our forefathers have started to revisit the land," Shankhaleima said, after a deep puff on the hubble-bubble. "Give offerings at the time of Pitripaksha with whatever your father-in-law was fond of. When Monigo is fast asleep, you have to spell thrice – 'Monigo stay in my womb, stay in my womb, stay in my womb...' Massage his body while chanting the words. Put a piece of broken twig from a broom by his bedside after the floor has been swept clean," Shankhaleima spelt out the remedy.

"Shankhaleima, oh Shankhaleima," came a call from the neighbouring house. Recognising the caller's voice she responds—"What's the matter, *boiji?*"

"The Khullakpa Lokei (Khullakpa clan) has invited you to invoke their forefathers to their *sradh* ceremony. They requested you to reach a bit early," the caller said.

"Yes, I will," Shankhaleima replied soberly, but bared her true sentiments before Taraleima. "She's much younger than I am," she fumed. "By virtue of being the widow of Kamara-dada, our neighbour, she is calling me by name, and that too, in a commanding tone."

"Kamara-dada married her at the fag end of his life; she is his third wife. This is why I call her *boiji.* She was a newly-wedded bride when your elder brother was a toddler. A young girl then, she was like a new toy for Kamara-dada"

A stunned Taraleima then questioned her mother. "Mother," she said—"You used to be quite happy when Githani aunt earlier called you by name. Why are you so annoyed now?"

"Why not? She could call me 'Kartiksena's mother' or 'Taraleima's mother' instead of using my name," an annoyed Shankhaleima replied.

"Mother, could you spell out what's done while calling the souls of forefathers?" Taraleima changed the subject.

"At the penultimate night of a sradh, with seven lighted wicks and an equal number of ceremonial offering of *eira tankha* one has to pray..." the mother explained to the daughter.

Taraleima made an attempt to strike a chord with her mother. "Mother," she said. "When will you tell me all about the herbal *pièce de résistance*, the cure-all, which was revealed to you in a dream?"

An unmoved Shankhaleima puffed away at the hookah.

"Why are you so reluctant to disclose the secrets of this traditional treasure? Who else is there besides me to inherit the knowledge? Will your daughter-in-law inherit them?" demanded Taraleima, sounding like an impetuous child asking for a special favour.

"All to yourself. Who else is there to inherit them? The time, however, isn't ripe," said the mother, puffing at the hubble-bubble yet again. Shankhaleima was a famous faith healer in the locality by virtue of the all-curing herb revealed to her in a dream. She wasn't ready to spill out the secret details of this herb, not even to her tenacious daughter. The herb has to be uprooted in one breath from a hill on a dark-moon night coinciding with a Saturday.

"Mother, if you take it with you when you go..."

"You stupid girl! I'm not a fool! I won't die without choosing an auspicious moment, mind it. My body will let me know the very moment of my demise. I'll have enough time to whisper to you the name of the herb. Mine isn't an ordinary body like yours. It has been totally shielded by my father with tantras. If need be, I can even defer death indefinitely," an enraged Shankhaleima told her daughter, clenching her teeth.

Frightened by the intense glare of her mother's grey eyes, Taraleima quickly concluded that her mother was truly a formidable occultist.

"Mother, why don't you shield my body too with tantras?" Taraleima asked next.

Their conversation was cut short by Madanchand's arrival. He parked his bicycle in the courtyard and glancing at the mother-daughter duo asked jestfully—"Taraleima, have you got the precious name of the all-cure herb revealed?"

"Aargh! There comes the spoilsport!" Shankhaleima scowled, resolutely going back to her hookah.

"Madanchand, why do you keep pulling my mother's leg? Could physicians cure your uncle's typhoid? Tell me, could the science you boast of cure him? Why do you forget that it was my mother's herb that cured him! " retorted an angry Taraleima.

"I agree, it's good. No offence meant. Just let me know when you get the name of the dream herb. I want to get my body shielded by you," a smiling Madanchand said casually, stepping into the house.

"Mother, this teacher has spelt doom for the two kids. It's this teacher who has made dada's views do a complete somersault," Taraleima told her mother.

"No my dear. Your sister-in-law is the culprit. She has made my son disobedient by working charms on him! My son was a rare gem among a thousand boys! He wouldn't dare go out alone on a Saturday dark-moon night without his mother accompanying him with a lamp. Before going to bed he would always shield his body by spelling out the mantras I had taught him. He was totally under my tutelage from the day I conceived him," Shankhaleima told Taraleima.

"Mother, I must be going now," Taraleima said and called Monigo who dragged himself away from the television with unwilling steps. Shankhaleima handed him a ripe guava. Stopping them near the courtyard, Shankhaleima asked them to wait. "It's too late, and the day too is an ominous one," she warned. "Who can say that the spirit haunting the kapok tree near that desolate abyss won't cast its ugly shadow on you? Monigo is under a spell of nightmares these days." Shankhaleima took some mustard and cotton seeds and some broken tips of a broomstick—all repellent to spirits.

"Here you go." Shankhaleima wrapped the repellents in two separate rags of her angaluri, and tied them on the arms of Manigo and Taraleima with reef knots[82]. Having had their bodies shielded, they left for home without any fear.

Madanchand was teaching Babashou the concept of the water cycle—

"Water of canals, lakes, rivers and other water bodies, turns into vapour and goes up in the sky. But why does it go up? Air becomes lighter when it is hot. At high altitude, it gets accumulated around dust particles forming droplets of water, and ultimately clouds. Clouds fall as raindrops."

"Sir, what leads to thunder before rain?" Babashou asked his teacher.

"Thunder occurs because water particles get charged electrically due to friction. When oppositely charged particles come closer, sparks are generated causing thunder and lightning," said the science teacher.

A puzzled Babashou frowned, looked at his sister and then at the teacher. In the meantime, the teacher started explaining to Imashou how lunar eclipse occurs. With the help of a diagram, Madanchand taught her how the shadow of the earth falls on the moon leading to lunar eclipse. Imashou got a clear concept of lunar eclipse. Babashou heard all of what the teacher taught

---

82 Reef knots: The *reef knot* or *square knot* is an ancient and simple binding knot used to secure a rope or line around an object. 'Right over left and left over right; makes a knot both tidy and tight' is a popular description of the knot.

his sister, saw the diagram drawn but failed to understand the phenomenon. Though he was eager to get a clear concept of lunar eclipse, he didn't feel like asking the teacher since it wasn't his lesson. He looked up the diagram in his book showing clouds falling as rain and water flowing down the river. He kept himself busy in drawing a frog predating a fish.

After the tutorial class, Madanchand went to watch news headlines on the TV along with Kartiksena and Gauri, while Imashou and Babashou rushed to their grandmother to listen to fairy tales.

"Grandma, sir has taught me what leads to lightning and thunder before the rains. Please tell us a tale," Babashou requested her. Shankhaleima was happy to be with her grandchildren. Earlier they would be with her almost round the clock just to hear tales, but since the time they started going to school and watching television, they seldom found time to be with her. Even then whenever they got time they had the habit of rushing to Shankhaleima. With her mesmerising art, Shankhaleima, raconteur, began telling them a story—

"It is believed that the sky was much closer to the earth many years ago. Our forefathers fondly called the sky, Douraja. There was a village under the sky. The children of the village used to frolic and play hide-and-seek amidst stars. They also used to enjoy storytelling by sitting on the tender moon. The old people, on the other hand, sat basking in the sun, chatting among themselves. It so happened one day that a woman of the village had a quarrel with her husband and was angry. She started to husk paddy in a big mortar with a tall and heavy pestle. Each time she raised the pestle, it hit the sky hard and each forceful stroke rattled the earth and the sky as well. The groaning sky began inching away from the earth, and finally drifted apart. Douraja got annoyed. He started to exhale hot air and growled. His exhaled air got condensed.

He started shouting with his eyes sparking. Thunder shook the earth and parched its surface. The catastrophe made the villagers gather under the sky. They scolded the woman and prostrated on the ground with hands folded to appease Douraja. They prayed to him to not be offended as the woman was oblivious of the mistake she had made. They all requested Douraja to come down and stop destroying the earth. They also took a pledge that they wouldn't do anything so impetuous in future."

The sky cooled down and stopped growling. He told the villagers: "Oh my dear fellows, I can only go up, but not come down. I shall be too far away to talk to you!"

"All good people of the village, including the children, began to sob. The wails of the children made Douraja shed incessant tears. Even now, when Douraja gets angry for not being able to play with children and give them presents, he gets angry. The hot air exhaled by him turns into cloud and his growl causes thunder and lightning. It rains when he sobs. Bishnu, Bishnu...[83]"

Shankhaleima entertained her grandchildren with the engaging tale. An enchanted Babashou was listening to the story, mouth wide open. He was unaware that under the magic spell of the tales he laid bare the vacant sockets of his two upper incisors. He stared at the sky, lying in the lap of his grandma and started playing hide and seek amidst the twinkling stars. Imashou, on the other hand, was looking at the dazzling moon. She asked Shankhaleima: "Grandma, what are the black patches seen on the surface of the moon?"

"Those are sacred and the rarest of rare herbs grown on the moon," Shankhaleima replied, much to the satisfaction of the girl.

"But what are those?" she asked the old woman again.

---

83 Bishnu, Bishnu...": Special style of signing off before finishing folktales in the name of Lord Vishnu.

"Those are herbs. Their leaves, when taken, make people immortal and evergreen," Shankhaleima elaborated.

"How can those herbs grow on the moon where there is no oxygen and water?" Imashou asked her Grandma. "That's another long story. I shall tell you that some other day," Grandma replied.

"You have to tell the story today. Our sir says that the spots are patches of the moon."

Imashou kept on requesting her grandmother. "It's forbidden topic. Bishnu Bishnu!" the old woman cautioned her.

Looking at the moon, Shankhaleima asked for divine blessings with her hands folded and ran her palms across her face. She then started the tale—

"It goes like this—many moons ago, a family of Alokgo Lokei (Alokgo clan) found some seeds of the herb that makes people immortal. They spread out the seeds for drying in a winnow in their courtyard under the sun before the next sowing season during monsoon. Their black mean-looking doggy, almost resembling a tiger was keeping vigil on the seeds without even blinking its eyes. Even the gods were scared of the gigantic canine.

"In one of his regular strolls on the Milky Way, Sarallel recognised the seeds. He was at a loss, not knowing what to do. He called other gods and showed them the seeds.

"'If human beings consume that herb, they will be immortal and remain evergreen like us. That will spell doom for us. We shouldn't let that happen,' Sorallel told other gods.

"The gods soon held a meeting, and asked the Sun God to transmit its scorching heat so as to make the doggy move away. The Sun did so. The dog moved closer to the winnow and lay down with its ears flopped low. When the move failed, the gods then asked Bouraja, the Storm God, to do something worthwhile. With a strong whirlwind, Bouraja took the seeds of the special herb away and placed them on the moon. However, the whirlwind flew the dog away too, in the sky where it floated in mid-air. Not being able to come down, the angry dog swallowed the moon and the sun alternately and released them, causing lunar eclipse and solar eclipse respectively. From the seeds grew a number of herbs on the moon's surface. The dark spots on the moon are the shadows of those herbs. If one consumes a leaf of the plant, he or she will remain immortal and evergreen. It's the best and only anti-ageing herb. Bishnu, Bishnu..."

"Where are you, Imashou and Babashou? Come and see how rockets are made. Hurry up! Watch the TV," shouted Gouri. The two siblings then rushed to the TV. All of a sudden, Shankhaleima felt deserted. She blamed it on the TV that continued to drive a wedge between her and her grandchildren. Looking at the moon for a long while she started to sing a philosophical song, "*Salo mon pahiya, ghar duwar beleya* (Oh, flying mind leave hearth and home and go in search of God)...."

*

On her way back home after calling the forefathers of the Khullakpa Lokei on the eve of a *sradh*, Shankhaleima came across Madanchand. He was bound for Shankhaleima's home to take the tutorial class of her grandchildren. He alighted from the bicycle and started walking alongside Shankhaleima.

"Grand-aunt, are you returning from the bereaved Khullakpa Lokei's house?" "Yes," Shankhaleima responded. Madanchand accompanied her on foot.

"You better go ahead, since you're with the bicycle," said Shankhaleima. "I'm not scared of any evil spirits. Mine is a sanctified body, shielded with tantra-mantra by my father. Evil spirits won't dare touch me," she said confidently.

"It's not that grand-aunt. I want to know something," Madanchand said.

"What do you want?" the old woman asked him.

"I heard from Imashou and Babashou that the herbs which immortalise people are on the surface of the moon. Is that so?" he questioned the grand old woman.

"And why not? You won't believe me, I know. Get lost," she told Madanchand.

"Don't be annoyed grand-aunt." Madanchand started appeasing her, adding, "A process is underway to set up a colony on the surface of the moon. Since there's no human being, people from the earth will be given the opportunity to settle down on the moon. A rocket will take off for the moon with people ready to settle down, from the earth."

Shankhaleima had already heard the news that people were going to the moon in rockets. "Madanchand isn't talking rubbish of course," she told herself, carefully but quietly listening to Madanchand, not uttering a single word.

"Cultivation of paddy has begun on the surface of the moon. Since America and England have no sowing experts, women experts in the job are being taken from Indian villages," Madanchand said.

A confused Shankhaleima looked at Madanchand, suffering the pangs of indecision and suspicion.

"My wife Shefalika believes that you were one of the best among sowers of paddy saplings in the village," Madanchand said.

"Shefalika is from the hamlet located next to ours. She might have seen me sowing paddy. She is a meek and a good lady," an overwhelmed Shankhaleima muttered.

"But you've had your day as a sower and reaper of paddy. Had you been slightly younger..." Madanchand said, provoking the dormant wishes embedded in her.

A beaming Shankhaleima soon rose to the bait, and said: "What do you say? You haven't yet discovered what kind of a woman I am! Even now nobody can challenge me in the field. I can sow a *bigha* of land within a few hours."

"There's an advantage if you go to the moon. Others can't identify the herb that makes people immortal and evergreen. But you can," Madanchand said.

"Why not? That's a divine herb, quite distinct from the rest," she replied.

"If two or three leaves of that herb can be brought here, you will get your youth back. Besides being immortal, Shefalika and I can remain evergreen as well," said Madanchand.

"You don't believe all these. Why is this about-turn? Are you making me a fool?" Shankhaleima questioned him.

"I swear grand-aunt. Whether I believe it or not, I don't want to grow old and die. What's the harm if I get good results from the herb? I certainly have faith in herbal medicines but not in black magic," Madanchand explained. Shankhaleima kept quiet. Her dull eyes brightened with a faraway dream, tinged with a fresh and bright verdant hue. Her eyes beamed with joy and hope. If only she could go to the moon and fetch a few leaves of the herbs...

Madanchand could gauge the impact of his trick on the woman. He stole a glance at Shankhaleima and smiled. Pretending that something serious was troubling him, Madanchand heaved a deep sigh, and said: "There's a problem grand-aunt."

"What?" Shankhaleima asked him.

'The security personnel deployed there will resort to thorough body search before people board the rocket from the earth and the moon. Bringing the leaves from practically under their nose will be really difficult," Madanchand said.

"I know all the tricks. I will simply tuck away a few leaves under my breasts. Let me go there first," Shankhaleima said.

Madanchand was sure that she had accepted the offer with alacrity.

"Okay, let me talk to the people operating the rocket ferry. But don't forget us after landing on the moon," Madanchand pulled her leg. He had successfully planted the story.

"What nonsense!" Shankhaleima retorted.

❋

Shankhaleima was determined to go to the moon, at any cost. By taking the leaves of the immortalising herb, she had to establish the fact that there was profound truth in what old people said and believed. She was ready to surprise the non-believers by regaining her youth. Her confidence had received a boost after what Madanchand had confided to her. Like every other day, Shankhaleima kept glancing at the moon. She discovered that the moon looked a bit different that day. The leaves of the immortalising herbs were quite distinct. The moon also seemed closer to her than usual. She firmly believed that as soon as she reached the moon's surface, she would eat a few leaves and play safe. Even if she failed to gift everybody the boon of rejuvenation, at least she would get her youth back. If she could bring some leaves back, who would she share them with?

Madanchand and Shefalika were on her priority list. She would give it to her son Kartiksena and daughter Taraleima, her grandchildren – Imashou, Babashou and Monigo – but not her daughter-in-law, Gouri. Shankhaleima continued to live with the agony that Gouri had snatched her beloved son away from her. Not to speak of the villagers, even her own daughter-in-law didn't trust her faith healing. She wasn't even respectful of the amulet revealed in a dream. "A traitor! Lost in the pride of your good looks! I will show you what beauty is and you shall see for yourself what I look like when I regain my youth," Shankhaleima muttered to herself.

Would Shankhaleima really deprive her daughter-in-law if she fell on her feet and begged? Gouri was her only daughter-in-law, chosen by none other than herself! Shankhaleima would surely consider.

*

Washing her hands of lust, greed and all other worldly pleasures, a hoary old Shankhaleima had been knocking on the door of renunciation, about to retire from her household life. Having conceived the dream of regaining youth, she didn't seem quite her usual self. An indolent lust started growing in her.

One morning, after her bath in the pond she walked to a champa tree. Instead of the usual ginger lilies, she put two champa flowers in her ears. While conducting her prayers near the basil plant in the courtyard, she fell into a trance and even forgot to drink basil water as usual, deep in thought and wondering whether Madanchand would really do enough to send her to the moon! Or would he send his wife alone? Was he to be trusted?

Would Shefalika be able to identify the wild immortalising plants? Shankhaleima wondered. Shefalika wouldn't go alone, leaving her behind. She was educated yet conservative when it came to folk beliefs. Polite manners were inborn. She bowed down respectfully to Shankhaleima wherever they met.

A restless Shankhaleima received Madanchand in the evening outside the house. "Any development?" she asked him anxiously.

Madanchand alighted from the bicycle, and said: "I've submitted an application in your name to the party ferrying people to the moon on rockets. Let's wait for the response."

"Only for me?" Shankhaleima asked. "Why not one for Shefalika?"

"What'll she do there?" Madanchand demanded to know. "She can't even identify a common herb, how can she identify the immortalising herb?"

'I'll be with her. Don't underestimate her. She is the daughter of an arbitrator of repute, Thabal Singh. She has also completed her college like you have," she said indignantly.

"Okay then. Since you insist, I'll submit another application for her," said Madanchand.

Hushed conversation between Madanchand and Shankhaleima continued for a few days. Once an eyesore, Madanchand transformed into her dearest and closest confidante. One day Madanchand informed Shankhaleima that their applications had been approved. From that very day, slowly but surely Shankhaleima started to arrange her clothes for the lunar holiday. Her ready set of white clothes found no room in her bags. There were only colourful dresses that she had worn as a teenager and a newly-married bride. Only one white dress for widows was packed in, to be worn while stepping out of home on the D-Day. She opened the bamboo basket and took out the folded talaphuti and the inafi, which held the flavours of her romantic days of youth perfectly in their folds. She unfolded the dress, held it against the light, folded it back and somehow tucked it into the tightly packed luggage.

"Dressed in these clothes, with two champa flowers in my ears after letting down my long black tresses reaching beyond the knees, when I descend from the moon after regaining youth, will the villagers be able to recognise me? Will Gouri recognise me at all? No, never. Of course, Kartiksena will. He has seen my beauty when he was quite young."

One day, after their evening study session, Imashou and Babashou rushed to Shankhaleima to hear stories from her.

"Grandma, please tell us a new story," her grandchildren requested her. Shankhaleima started telling them a story that she had planned.

"Once upon a time, there was an Alokgo Lokei lass. She was very choosy in selecting a groom for herself. She became a spinster with wrinkles and veins. Finding no way out, her father called Sarallel with devotion. Satisfied at the call of his devotee, Sarallel put down his golden ladder from heaven for the girl and her father. They made no delay to ascend to heaven. Bowing down to Sarallel, the poor father said: "You are our God. You have created all these creatures and scripted their fates. You have created my daughter and scripted her fate too. Who is her match, according to your scripture? We failed to find him out, and that led me to approach you, me lord.'"

After a patient hearing, Sarallel said: "You fool. Already a yuga has elapsed on the earth since you came to me. When you return, nobody will recognise you as his ancestor. Okay then, let me help your daughter." Saying so, Saralel handed over a leaf of the immortalising herb to the girl, and said: "On your way back home, eat this leaf after a holy dip in a river. You will regain your youth. Your groom will come to you on his own."

They bowed down to Sarallel, and came down the ladder. The village looked quite new to them, and nobody could recognise them. Before reaching home, the girl took a bath in a river and took the leaf. Within a few moments, she became a tender and svelte girl, in her early teens. Her complexion resembled the wild banana flower, her breasts took the shape of a pair of identical wood apples and her waist was as slim as a cane. Her father was overjoyed seeing his daughter.

The villagers were a strange lot. They couldn't recognise them, but when they narrated their ancestry, their descendants had to go through their list of forefathers inscribed on a bamboo piece that was preserved for *tarpan*[84], and found the name of the father of the girl. Their descendants welcomed them to their residence. Youths from various areas made a beeline to tie the knot with the girl, who, however, refused to choose any of them. One day when the girl was having a bath in a river with other girls of the village, Sarallel saw her from the sky overhead. A stunned Sarallel kept on looking at the girl, and said to himself: "What a beautiful girl! How could such a girl be on the earth?" He couldn't hold himself back and came down to the bank of the river. All the girls bowed down to him. He praised the girl: "You look like a fairy. Who are you? What's your name?"

"Oh my lord, can't you recognise me? I'm that girl whom you have given the leaf of the immortalising herb. My name is Madoi," the girl replied in her sweet voice.

"Oh, I see. Call your father. I would like to marry you," an enchanted Sarallel said.

"Grandma, you had told us the tale of Madoi-Sarallel earlier. Have you forgotten? Today's tale has a lot of new twists which weren't there in the earlier story. Are these new additions? Today's tale is not at all interesting," Babashou complained and left and so did Imashou.

"A good riddance!" Shankhaleima thought to herself and laughed aloud. She wished to be left alone so that she could spend some time with herself and her wild imagination. Who knew what life held in store for her. After regaining youth, even Sarallel could be... Who can rule out that she wouldn't meet Sarallel on her way back home from the moon? She cherished in her mind an encounter like that of Madoi-Sarallel and kept herself engrossed with that unsaid end of the tale.

---

84 *Tarpan*: Offering of homage to the forefathers to appease their souls.

That night, Shankhaleima couldn't sleep at all. She kept tossing and turning in bed. Riding on fresh hopes and aspirations, she took a trip down memory lane. She would regain her youth, but her husband was not alive. Would she get him back? Had he been alive, she would have made him get his youth back. In her regained youth, who would be Shankhaleima's paramour? Would that lead to marriage? No, not again. She wouldn't mother children again. What's the result of giving birth to a baby after keeping it in the womb for nine months? What's the outcome of bringing a child up by reducing the self to a skeleton? When they grow up, they forget everything. She wouldn't marry again, not even Sarallel.

She held on firmly to her decision of not leaving the village. She would stay put in the village like Rambha, Menoka and the other celestial beauties. The young men of the village would surely make a beeline for her, but whom would she get her claws into? Dholamanu, Hunashou, Dhananjay or Samir? During the sleepless night, she grew sixty-three years younger. Her mind went back to her heady days of matchmaking and her passions rose to a high. She recalled how Senatol had touched her body for the first time on the pretext of smearing colours on her face during Holi. She recalled Baladeb's delaying tactics to make full use of his secret tryst with her while dressing her in full regalia as a Gopi for a Raasleela. She still remembered the tight hug by Harikumar, dressed like a knight in shining armour, on the pretext of rescuing her, a damsel in distress, from under the boat. The boat had capsized in a regatta on the occasion of Janmashtami. The fond memories of the bridal bed that she had shared with Tamphasena continued to return to her mind and colour her dreams.

*

One day Madanchand rushed to the community pond, called Shankhaleima there and said, "The rocket will take off this evening, Grandma. I've to hurry as Shefalika is accompanying you. If you're to go, you have to reach the hill near the grazing ground on time. The rocket will land there. It won't wait. Can you?" Madanchand asked her.

Shankhaleima's eyes beamed and her entire being was electrified. Dumbstruck with joy, she could only nod her head.

"I don't have any tuition to give your grandchildren today. So I've informed you of the news now," Madanchand said, riding away on his bicycle. After paddling hard for some time, he got off the bicycle at a sharp bend and stood behind a Gokul tree, keeping a watch on the old woman. Shankhaleima took a long bath; scrubbing her body with an organic loofah, swimming and playing in the water. She plucked some champa flowers and with her body still wet, ran back home, as though she was still in her teens.

The slow sinking sun made her restless and impatient. The fiery ball of light seemed to be clinging to the banyan tree like a bat on the rear side of the village, reluctant to let go. In the evening, like every other day, Taraleima came and offered her mother the hookah and soon left for home after exchanging a few words, finding her mother in no mood to prolong the conversation. Shankhaleima kept her mission a secret from her daughter. She'd rather die than betray Madanchand.

Later, she sat on the threshold watching the news bulletin telecast on TV. She saw the rocket just launching, ejecting smoke profusely, much to the joyous clapping of Imashou and Babashou. An elated Shankhaleima went to the courtyard and looked up at the full moon. She didn't feel like singing any philosophical song and instead, asked Gauri to prepare dinner earlier than usual on the pretext of getting hungry. She asked her to cook a quick, small meal—an *erolpa* with long beans and a brinjal fry. She herself took the matchet and started to process vegetables.

Babashou and Imashou approached Shankhaleima with their request of a story. With her mind obsessed with the dream of regaining youth, Shankhaleima was in no mood to tell a story. Softly caressing them, she said, "I don't have any story to tell you today. It's an off-day for me. Why don't you grant me leave today? Go to bed early after your meal. I shall tell you a fine story after a few days."

"What's the story about, Grandma? Can't you tell it today?" Babashou implored.

"Even I myself don't know the story that I should tell you today," Shankhaleima confessed.

"Okay Grandma, tell us the story tomorrow," said Babashou.

"Not tomorrow."

"Why? Tomorrow isn't your off day."

"Sorry dear, after a few days, say after..." Shankhaleima was lost in uncertainty. How many days would she be on the moon?

The upset grandchildren went back crestfallen to watch TV. A relieved Shankaleima smiled and thanked them silently.

"By what name shall these two grandchildren of mine call me when I come back from the moon, a pretty young girl...?"

The family had a quick supper and went to bed; the household fell almost silent. While Imashou and Babashou soon fell asleep, one could still hear pillow talk in soft tones between Kartiksena and Gauri. Shankhaleima, on the other hand, kept her luggage near her pillow on the bed and waited impatiently for her son and daughter-in-law to fall asleep.

As time went by, Shankhaleima became restless. Finally she concluded that Kartiksena was fast asleep as he was snoring deeply. Gauri was also silent. At last the rest of the household fell deeply asleep. Shankhaleima rose, sat on the bed, and climbed down. Attired in a snow-white angaluri and an inafi, she took her luggage, spelled slowly thrice from the bed — arise, arise, arise — bowed down at the corner of the house meant for Senamahi, opened the door quietly and finally came out to the verandah. She took the old and seasoned stick used by her late husband from the roof. At eighty, though she wasn't normally using any stick. She had to take the stick now to drive away stray dogs. She tested the free passage of air through her nostrils and stepped out from the verandah for the moon mission. The full moon night was particularly bright and this made Shankhaleima apprehensive of being noticed. Their pet dog came barking from the cowshed. With teeth clenched in anger, she drove away the dog with the stick. The dog obeyed her and kept silent. She bowed down before the basil plant, marked a chandan tilak on her forehead with the wet soil beneath the plant and left for the house of Madanchand cautiously, avoiding the patter of her footsteps. Their faithful dog accompanied her as the only escort. She made an attempt to drive the canine away, but to no avail.

"These are some of the hurdles on the way to a good mission. It seems as if this pet is more affectionate towards me than my son and grandchildren," she murmured to herself.

Shankhaleima was panting heavily when she reached the gate of Madanchand as she had to race against time. Madanchand's dog started barking with its hackles raised so as to scare away the dog escorting Shankhaleima.

"Madanchand, o Madanchand. Shefalika, o Shefalika," Shankhaleima whispered in a husky voice. The barking dogs and the loud whispers of Shankhaleima woke both Madanchand and Shefalika: "Shankhaleima Grandma!" Shefalika told Madanchand.

"I told you many a time not to play a trick on this simple old woman for amusement. This isn't fair. What will you do now?" an annoyed Shefalika asked Madanchand, who simply said: "It was beyond my imagination that she'd come here in the middle of the night on foot."

"It's okay. You don't believe in mantra and faith-healing. You just have faith in science. Only science and technology can't make society run smoothly. You have to keep in mind that folk beliefs too are an important component of a community," she tried to explain.

"Atoms and molecules don't constitute a community," Shefalika continued. A society is made up of human beings. Had you studied social sciences like I did, you would have had the idea of what role such folk beliefs play in society," Shefalika said firmly, as she was very upset about Madanchand playing a trick with Shankhaleima.

"Now go and make the old woman understand what you have done," she said. Madanchand hung his head, struck by sudden repentance. He tendered an abject apology to Shefalika. "Yes, I've committed a crime," he murmured. "What you say is right. How can I go and face grand-aunt? I need your help to get the old woman forgive me."

"It's I, Madanchand, it's I who has been calling you," Shankhaleima called out in a clear voice as she thought that the couple was taking time to open the door because they had not been able to identify her. Shefalika took a quick look at her husband, the one who had always held his head high, and who now hung his head in shame. She rose from the bed and opened the door.

"What! Haven't you got ready as yet? The rocket will land now. That won't wait for us. Get dressed, hurry up," Shankhaleima said. The sight of the oldest woman in the hamlet – endowed with the rich knowledge of folklore, ancient folk culture and dying traditions of a very select group of ethnic people, dressed in a snow-white angaluri and an inafi, waiting at their door in the bright moonlit night with much expectation – made tears tricke down Shefalika's cheeks. Without uttering a single word, she bowed down to her.

"What are you doing? Shefalika, what are you doing? Get up my child!" Shankhaleima, stunned beyond words, said falteringly.

"Grandma, please forgive him," Shefalika said slowly, holding on tightly to the feet of Shankhaleima, washing them with her tears. Mandanchand too came out and joined Shefalika, muttering in awkward penitence: "Grand-aunt, I've committed a sin. Forgive me, if you can."

Their plea left Shankhaleima dumbfounded. She stood still and stared at the couple. She understood the implicit meaning of these words. Her bright smiling face, hitherto beaming with the dream of the moon mission, suddenly fell, turning pale and wrinkled. Her demeanour instantly switched over to that of a bent and shrivelled old woman, cutting a sorry, pitiful figure. Hot tears pricked her eyes.

"Oh, God! I've understood..." Her voice choked with emotion. The pair of flowers in her long earlobes bobbed up and down. She looked down to see the couple grovelling at her feet, by supporting her bodyweight on the stick she held in her hand. She touched the tops of Madanchand's and Shefalika's heads with her right hand, and softly said, "Get up. It's okay. May God grant you a happy life."

Shankhaleima looked up at the full moon. The immortalising herbs were more distinct than ever. She closed her steadily misting eyes and prayed to the moon. Two drops of hot tears poured down her cheeks to the ground and got soaked into the earth in no time. She turned back, not knowing how to face her friends and family. Her son, daughter-in-law and other villagers might have started looking for her. What would she tell her inquisitive little grandchildren—Imashou and Babashou?

Shankhaleima took a step homewards and lost her balance, her head going dizzy and light. The stick fell to the ground. Shefalika was quick to catch her and check the fall. Madanchand picked up the stick and handed it over to her. They accompanied her up to their gate. Shefalika stopped there. Madanchand, however, continued to accompany her.

"It's fine. I can go. Leave me alone, please. Where's my stick?" Octogenarian Shankhaleima trudged back home with doddering strides. Weighed down by the bright glow of a clear full-moon night, she staggered and stooped low. The good old dog sniffed around her feet, walking past her every minute only to come back, keep her company and escort her.

GOD FOR A NIGHT

At Gokul

*T*he Rasolila[85] is slated for the forthcoming Rasopurnima. The villagers crowd around Hoba's house day in, day out. And that's not without reason. It's the only Rasolila of the year in the entire *porgona*[86]. Back from arduous harvest, the villagers simply flock to Hoba's house soon after lunch to enjoy Rasolila in rehearsal. A mammoth gathering on the D-Day is on the cards. Hoba is on cloud nine. The passionate wish for holding a Rasolila at home and playing the role of Brinda has gnawed at her heart since adolescence. She is no mean artiste herself. She has been Brinda in Rasolila and Nandarani in Rakhual many a time, even after her marriage. But were they one and the same—dancing in the Rasolila organised by others and playing the lead role in one's own?

She is determined to host the grand Rasolila. A decade has already gone by after her marriage. Monigo is going to be nine years old. Good Lord! The event has surely been delayed! Now Monigo too can play the role of a youthful Krishna. Maybe, this is why Monigo's father has delayed hosting the event.

Rasdhari Oja Guna comes every evening for the rehearsal and returns late at night. He slogs his guts out for the Rasolila.

---

85 Rasolila: A dance drama depicting Lord Krishna's night-long tryst with Sri-Radha and other *gopis*.
86 *Porgona*: A sub-district drawn out of a cluster of hamlets.

All's not well for him—the harvesting of paddy, barring his, is over; the D-Day is approaching fast and the *gopis* aren't too much at ease with some of the new songs. To top it all, the lad playing Krishna is far more interested in games than in dance. Besides his devil-may-care attitude, the boy cooks up diverse pretexts to skip rehearsals. The villagers have long been waiting for this traditional and joyous ceremony. Keeping that in mind, Oja Guna drops by at Hoba's house once in the morning too, on his way to the field. He drinks his early morning cuppa at Hoba's house.

So as usual, after downloading two sheaths of paddy, Oja Guna is on his way to the field today en route Hoba's house, singing the newly composed songs, drumming his fingers on the wooden pole resting on his shoulder. Monigo's father appears, cleans the settee in the verandah, receives the oja and bows down to him. Hoba too bows and greets the oja and sits down.

"Hey Monigo! Go and get a bundle of bidi and some tea leaves from the shop, pronto!" Manu tells his son from the verandah. No sooner has Manu taken out a repeatedly folded five-rupee note from his waistband; Monigo closes his book and rushes to the verandah with a flying leap from inside the house. He has a toy muroli[87] in hand. He has been nursing it round the clock, since the day the rehearsal for the Rasolila got underway. His oja too, doesn't let him be without the muroli for a moment. And this is one diktat that Monigo follows unfailingly, though the same can't be said for others!

Literally snatching the five-rupee note from his father, he picks up a bicycle ring propped against the reed wall of the house and leaves for the shop of Madhu-grandpa, rolling the ring, holding the muroli in his left hand.

---

87 *Muroli*: The flute of Lord Krishna (*murali* in Sanskrit).

"Don't be late. You'll have to go to school," Hoba says.

"Yes Ima."

Reaching the village road, Monigo looks back at his home, hidden behind the sprawling banyan tree. Switching the muroli to his right hand, he starts steering the ring by using the flute as the handlebar.

Hoba rehearses the staves of a new song on the verandah, under the careful guidence of the oja. Mesmerised with the songs, Manu cleans the cowshed, quite drowned in the soulful melody. Manu, Monigo's father, is known in the entire porgona to be a skinflint of sorts.

Will the niggardly man, who sells his own cow's milk – leaving not a drop for his household – really hold the extravaganza? This is a common query doing the rounds of the village. Hoba, on the other hand, is not ready to buy their comment at its face value. She has been keeping her hopes alive for around ten years. She is well aware of the miserly streak in Manu from the day of their engagement. This is why she has let her mother control the purse strings for the Rasolila. However, by virtue of being his wife she has also discovered in Manu what their neighbours haven't and realised the reason behind this miserly trait. Manu's father had been an *esulpa*[88] of fame, but had lived in penury. He had no land, barring his home plot. This wasn't all the misery which lay in store for the family though! Losing his father at a tender age, Manu had to give up his studies and get on with life...sharing it with his lunatic mother. It was his plight in his early years that had turned him into a miser.

What stands in total contrast to what is whispered beyond his earshot is his passion about music and culture. He attends

---

88 *Esulpa*: A traditional singer.

rasolilas, *kirtons* and other socio-cultural functions and doles out money – however small an amount – as a token gesture of love and passion for performing artistes. These subtle gestures from Manu made Hoba collect her courage together and disclose to her husband her dream of holding a Rasolila at home, a hope that she had been nurturing for years. Manu never brushed aside her proposal. He assured her of holding the Rasolila at an opportune time, cash flow permitting. Now he was keeping his long-standing promise—and in dead earnest!

Monigo comes back soon. His is a whirlwind errand. Steering the bicycle ring with the right hand he holds the muroli in the left. He hands over the bundle of bidis and the small change to his father, props the bicycle ring against the wall and walks to his mother who is busy rehearsing songs, keeping beat on the ground with her bare palm.

Not stopping to speak, Hoba gestures at Monigo, asking him to keep the small packet of tea leaves in the kitchen. Monigo sprints to the kitchen.

Hoba follows soon after, the staves of the song getting over. She finds him doing exactly what she had been worrying over. In the throes of hunger, her son has already sneaked up to the little bowl of milk she had saved and finished it in one gulp. He was now licking the cream off his fingers. Picking up a big ladle lying nearby, Hoba runs after Monigo. The mother-son duo run around the hearth for a while till finally Monigo – much faster on his feet – manages to leave the house, all the while aping his mother with the flute. Hoba chases him, hot on his heels, finally catching hold of him near their pond and hitting him hard. Monigo begins sobbing uncontrollably.

"What's wrong?" Manu shouts across.

"Oh, nothing really. You needn't know everything," she replies brusquely.

"Such harsh treatment for a young lad who's just run an errand...! Have you done anything wrong, Monigo?" Manu pats his son's head in an effort to console him but the kind action brings forth a fresh stream of tears followed by loud wailing.

"Enough child, now be off to school, or else you'll be late," says Manu.

Monigo continues to cry by the pond. Hoba returns with two cups of tea, one for Manu and the other for the guest. She hovers around the guest and mumbles apologetically: "Oja, it's black tea. The little milk that I kept last night has turned sour."

*

At Sondipon Gurukul

After a long spell of crying, Monigo leaves for school.

"Come home immediately after classes break. Don't just keep loitering in the village," Hoba warns from home.

For Monigo, his mother remains to be an eternal mystery. Performing Nandarani's role in Gosthalila[89] she cries her heart out while singing about her young boy Krishna pilfering others' cream. On the other hand, she beats her only son, who plays the young Krishna in her Rasolila, with a big ladle just for polishing off a bit of cream from their home kitchen!

He finds none of his classmates on the road. Is it late? Walking faster, he stops near the public pond, in front of Gauro grandpa's house, noticing their teacher Karna Singh approaching from the opposite direction. Monigo's mouth feels as dry as a bone. The powerful head teacher of the lower primary school, Karna

---

89 Gosthalila: The life events of child Krishna in Gokul or Gostha.

Singh is a Goliath of a man. He resembles the mighty Karna of the *Mahabharat*. The bow-legged teacher has a foot-long face, a raised nose and hands almost reaching the knees. He can easily reach his hands out and box the ears of his students standing at a distance, making them see stars in the process.

Karna Singh doesn't just teach a class but serves his pupils with his presence and vigilance. Discipline is his middle name. Soon after the class roll call, when other teachers settle down in their respective classes, the headmaster makes a round of the homes of all the absent pupils with a cane in hand to ascertain the true reason behind their absence. If an absentee is really sick, he has no cause for worry. The headmaster is however, a real ogre for the truants. Those who try to hide from his roving eyes have to bear the brunt of it. He combs through every nook and cranny of homes and even roadside ditches, bringing all truants to school—come hell or high water.

Much to his relief, Monigo finds his teacher without his cane and attendance registers. A small brass pot in one hand and the sacred thread dangling from the right ear, he seemed on the other hand, to be on his way to the public pond for his morning ablutions and bath. Monigo heaves a sigh of relief. He surely wasn't late for school since the headmaster was coming for his bath! Rather he is much ahead of others. "Oja *namaskar*," Monigo wishes his teacher with confidence. The muroli is clutched between his folded hands.

The teacher stops and stares at Monigo, his eyes wide. "You Lord Krishna, come here," he calls Monigo. Taken aback, Monigo inches towards the teacher, maintaining a safe distance all the while. He looks around for help.

"You have wished me now, but never do this in future when I'm not dressed. Don't you see that I'm on my way to the pond to take a dip? Do you wish to drown me in the mirky depths of sin, boy? Go on straight to school. I shall follow soon. You know what punishment awaits you if you don't!" the teacher warns. Monigo sprints straight to school, which is on the bank of the horseshoe lake—perhaps the most beautiful spot in the village.

Before noon Oja Karna Singh brings the truants to school by their ears in droves. Bana and others, who are busy playing hopscotch in the front yard of the school after the tiffin break, quickly sneak away. Monigo, playing marbles with his mates in the verandah, drops the marbles in his pocket and stands quietly, leaning against a post.

Keeping the registers in the wooden almirah inside the ofiice, Oja Karna Singh comes out. Raising his right hand, he says: "Children, sit in rows in the front yard. Today we have three clusters of ripe bananas for you."

The pupils rush giggling to the front yard and sit in neat rows. Malati madam and Snehalata madam distribute the bananas, while the head teacher stands by, holding bunches of the fruit. He too smiles, seeing the kids enjoying the ripe fruits.

"Eat up kids. It's all yours," he announces cheerfully, his eyes feasting on the pleasant scene.

Oja Karna Singh. This was the man, with his steadfast belief in the purity snd simplicity of children's hearts. The villagers could ill afford to send their children to school packed with tasty and nutritious snacks. The head teacher, blessed with green fingers, grew bananas in the school compound. A natural horticulturist, Karna Singh lovingly looked after his plants and trees and worked in this tiny patch of green after school hours. Such feasts often came the children's way when bunches of bananas turned sunny yellow and ripe.

The head teacher smiles with delight as the children enjoy the bananas, almost like a child happy with his own creation.

*

Ding-dong, ding-dong...goes the bell. All the children in the school rush to their classrooms. The head teacher and Snehalata madam are on their way to the classes. Two classes are without teachers today and everybody tries to guess who of the two would come to their class. Putting all speculation to rest, the head teacher steps in and they all stand up to wish him. Monigo is a regular backbencher in class.

"Take your seats. You have arithmetic now. What lesson does your Tanu sir take these days?"

"Multiplication, sir."

"Any homework?"

"Yes sir. Sir had asked us to learn the multiplication table up to ten by heart," chants Badan, one of the frontbenchers.

Poor Monigo is a bundle of nerves.

"Right then. You recite the table of four; now you there— off with your table of eight," the teacher asks the students, one after another.

Monigo's heart thumps louder with the head teacher, finally turning his attention to the back benches.

"Over to you, Monigo!"

A nervous, shaking Monigo stands up.

"Tell me the table of seven."

"Oja, with the rehearsal for Rasolila underway, I haven't learnt that by heart. I'll tell you tomorrow, promise", Monigo tries to excuse himself, with the age-old pretence of crying. He steals a quick, furtive glance at the teacher.

Oja Karna Singh extends his hands up to Monigo's ear, giving the lad goose pimples.

"Oja, I'm holding it myself." Monigo keeps the muroli pressed against his armpit, holds his ears and stands up on the bench.

✳

On the banks of the Yamuna

After school hours Monigo is a king. Yes, a king indeed. He goes running to the front hamlet to play, with some of his classmates close behind. Monigo, backbencher in the classroom, is a leader of his agegroup outside the class – be it in wrestling, making bulls fight or trespassing on private orchards. He crosses the embankment and races through the standing sugarcane crop on the banks of the river, closely followed by his accomplices. In no time, they break two stems of sugarcane, hide themselves among the tall standing crops and rips the juicy strands apart with their teeth. The boys' gang then comes out of the crops.

On their way back home, they stand under the guava tree of Babasena grandpa—known for his meanness. With the tree standing well inside the high fencing, there is little scope of climbing it. Only three or four branches are visible beyond the fence. Monigo spots the few guavas he had seen the other day. They have turned yellow. He asks his accomplices to be ready and lobs the flute at the ripe guavas. He never misses the target. His accomplices are smart enough to catch the fruits, leaving the flute for him. A few more ripe guavas catch his attention. He throws the flute again. A number of guavas fall like nine pins, but his accomplices fail to catch them this time.

"Who's there? You just wait!" Babasena comes out with a curved and handy stick, woken rudely from his afternoon nap by the sounds. The gang rushes towards the school with the guavas and stands under a plum tree, near the bank of the lake. Barring them, the plum tree is devoid of owners. The tree has just started flowering. The fruits of the tree never get a chance to ripen, thanks to the young band of gluttons. Sitting there in relative safety, the boys start nibbling and gnawing at the ill-begotten guavas.

"Monigo, your Radha is coming. She's about to start the Rasolila here!" one of Monigo's friends nudges him.

Nibbling at a guava, Monigo turns back. A young girl – Bana – approaches them, walking along the side of the lake, singing and dancing by herself.

"*Jamuna puline, srirasomondolirmaje...e... e... e...*" goes the song. Oblivious to the fact that she is lagging much behind her schoolmates, she is engrossed in her dance, taking much care to express the subtle nuances of movement. The schoolbag hanging from her left shoulder also dances in rhythm.

The boys burst out laughing when she is about to reach the plum tree.

Taken aback, Bana stops still and looks all around. None of her mates seems to be around. She looks at those sitting under the plum tree.

"Radha is coming ... coming," they all tease her in chorus. A hesitant Bana awkwardly glances at them and spots Monigo sitting and eating guavas, with his back towards her. She breathes easy and drops to the ground near Monigo with a smile.

"Why have you come here? Your friends have gone far. Go with them," says Monigo.

Ignoring Monigo's words the girl closes up to him. Monigo's face expresses a certain amount of uneasiness. "Wow! They have started the Rasolila," the boys scream in chorus, moving around Monigo and Bana. Monigo pushes Bana aside roughly, and starts nibbling at a guava, leaning against the plum tree. The boys continue to tease Bana. They start shoving her hard towards Monigo. She is pushed and pressed to the ground. She starts crying.

"Why do you tease her?" Monigo closes up to Bana and yells at his mates. "Why have you pushed her so hard? What would you have done if she had fallen into the lake?" Monigo scolds the boy who had pressed Bana to the ground. He hits the boy with his flute. A deafening silence follows. In his bid to appease Bana, Monigo gives her a ripe guava – the right balm.

"Let's go home," he beckons her.

All of them are bound for their homes, taking a short cut across the field. Since the time the villagers have started setting their cattle free for grazing, Monigo and Co refuse to take the usual path.

"Coming with us or going through the meandering village path? There are razor-sharp blades of straw on the way. You can come at your own risk," Monigo tells Bana and steps on to the field. Others follow in his steps. Lagging behind, Bana follows them, gleaning clusters of paddy left behind by reapers.

Monigo halts in the middle of the field, so do his friends. The bull belonging to Kanchan-khura[90] with humped shoulders is sharpening its fighting skills by goring a ridge. That of Buldung-khura, on the other hand, is grazing at the other end of the field. Monigo rushes to bring back Buldung's bull while his friends bring that of Kanchan. As soon as it comes near his counterpart, the bull of Buldung-khura runs away. Monigo canes the bull with the muroli so as to make it stand face to face with the other bull which is busy chasing its opponent. All the boys struggle hard to block all escape routes. The fleeing bull is forced to slow down. The bull of Kanchan-khura attacks the other with a powerful head butt. The raised dust makes Bana stiffen in fear. Monigo forgets everything else during the bullfight, his daily source of amusement.

As time goes by, a nervous Bana is scared stiff. She implores Monigo to accompany her to the rehearsal but her requests fall on deaf ears.

---

90 Khura: Uncle.

"It's the last day of our rehearsal. If we're late, the elders will be out to look for us. If they find us so far away, there'll be trouble," says Bana.

All of a sudden, Monigo remembers what her mother had told him while leaving for school.

"Off I go!" Without waiting for the others, Monigo starts rushing back home. Bana, nimble on her feet, closely follows Monigo with gleaned clusters of paddy in her hands and her school bag dancing on her shoulder.

Homecoming

Rasolila is to be held the next day. Hoba's courtyard is teeming with villagers. Oja Guna is a gifted artiste who marches in to the beat of a different drummer. The drumbeat sounds like staccato bursts of gunfire. The back-up *mridongo*[91] player sweats profusely. Between counting musical measures, the oja hammers the song into the *sutradhari*[92] *patoli*'s head and gives Hoba tips on dance. The oja's voice is hoarse with exhaustion. The rehearsal continues in the right sequence—the dance of Radha's close companion Brinda followed by the dance of Krishna and the rest of the usual dance events involving the Radha-Krishna couple.

The villagers enjoy the rehearsal, sitting around quietly. Oja Karna Singh, arbitrator Thabal and some other elders sit there too. They have received the invitation for tomorrow's divine feast. Young men and women stand and watch the rehearsal,

---

91 *Mridongo (Mridanga)*: A percussion instrument accompanying devotional music—a large egg-shaped drum with a hollow earthen body with drumheads at both ends, one smaller than the other. Originates from West Bengal, Assam and Manipur.

92 *Sutradhari*: The main singer in Rasolila.

children and married women enjoy the show while sitting along the edge of the verandah.

An assiduous Manu – Hoba's husband – races against the clock. The wallet bound tightly with his waistband jumps with the drumbeat, in keeping with the pace of his killing schedule. He collects his grazing cattle and ties them to the posts in their shed with his eyes set on the road. Costumes for the Rasolila are still to arrive. Between finishing domestic chores and helping those erecting the pandal, he doesn't have much time to play host to the visitors. With Hoba busy rehearsing, it is his duty to look after those who have gathered. "Have you offered tea to oja and others?" He asks the girls who lend a helping hand willingly. Offering bidi to the elders sitting there, he rushes to the pandal. The tight-fisted Manu has changed into a large-hearted man for the sake of the Rasolila. After the Krishna dance, the gopis led by Radha stand in a circular line-up. The Radha-Krishna pair however, proves to be difficult to set up. Monigo feels ill-at-ease at the proximity of Bana and gives her a push; he doesn't allow her to stand near him while the girl sobs pitifully. In spite of his father Manu's requests Monigo says, "I won't dance if she does that again," and moves to the end of the courtyard. Finally he climbs to the top of the hay stack and sits tight.

The sutradhari begins the song. She is followed by the gopis. Oja Guna plays the mridongo with real enthusiasm. Two gopis start fanning Radha-Krishna. But the pair refuses to participate. Krishna sits on top of the haystack and Radha lies in the lap of her mother. The rehearsal continues and once the solo dance of Krishna is over, nobody pays him any attention. He lapses into a sulky silence, shredding the hay and beating them down with the flute. Only Bana blinks at him, their eyes meet frequently and they both make faces at each other, Monigo raising the flute in a mock gesture of hitting Bana with it.

As soon as the rehearsal ends, the dresser from Baromuni arrives with the dresses. Hoba unrolls two mats on the verandah, the dresses are laid out and women flock around, keen to see the costumes.

"We need to see *polleis*[93] before sunset," they clamour.

Wiping the sweat from his face after a drink of water, the man unties the package. The glittering outfits – *polleis, khongnams, khowals, mukuts, meikhums* – roll out on the mats. Reflections of smiling faces, including that of Bana, appear in the mirror-studded polleis. The distribution begins, much to the joy of the waiting crowd.

Bana is elated to have received her pollei. Nobody knows when Monigo has slipped down from the haystack. He quietly moves around, pretending to have no interest in the pollei, *khongnam* and the rest of the glitzy costumes. Twirling the flute in his right hand he sometimes steals a glance to locate his pollei in the whole lot. Hoba finally pulls him to her lap, makes him sit and gives him his dress—the *dhora*, the *chura, khowals, ghungurs* and the rest of it.

Finally, people leave for their homes with their polleis, after bidding farewell to Oja Guna, Oja Karna Singh and other elders sitting there. Monigo and Bana can't stop giggling with delight, eyeing the dresses of each other.

"Bow down to the teachers and elders," Hoba orders them.

Bana and Monigo bow down to Oja Guna, Oja Karna Singh and other elders who give them their blessings.

Monigo and Bana bow down to each of their parents too.

With her emotions running high, Hoba hugs Bana and Monigo together and sobs uncontrollably. Wiping her eyes, she

---

93 *Pollei*: The main garment of the regalia for Rasolila.

manages to say: "You two have to act as the pivot of the Rasolila tomorrow. You should dance with full sincerity and passion."

Like every other night while Bana follows her parents home, dancing all the way, Monigo sits near Oja Guna.

At 'nikunja van'

On rasopurnima night the village and its households are aglow with decorative lamps. The bright rasomondoli stands in the middle of the mandap. It's a creation of great artistic merit, crafted out of white paper and white thread—a paradise on earth for a night. Yes, it is indeed a wonderfully blissful and beauteous paradise set amidst the harsh reality of life! The mandap is filled to capacity.

The programme begins. Brinda dances to the rhythm of Manipuri music. An enthusiastic Oja Guna plays the mridongo with undivided attention and passion. The ringlets on his forehead toss about and dance along. The oja's skill in playing the mridongo and the sutrodhari patoli's skill in playing the mandila[94] put each other to the test. Any discordant note in the musical measure is heaven-forbidden. An alert patoli doesn't even get the respite to swallow the betel juice.

"*Tatta gindhen tagin dhenta, dhinta gindhen tagin dhen...*" Hoba keeps pace with the notes of the music. The emotional Vaishnavite audience is mesmerised at her performance. Hoba is naturally good looking; with the glittering pollei, meikhum and the jewellery from Baromuni her beauty has been enhanced. In the stillness of the night, even the full moon stops to stare at Hoba, dancing in the rasomondoli. Enthralled by the performance,

---

94 Mandila: Small hand-held cymbals strung together, played mainly with devotional music in eastern and north-eastern India.

Manu falls into a trance. He is back to his senses when he recalls the next character to appear in the line-up—the Krishna dance. Where's Krishna? Realising that his son was nowhere to be seen, Manu rushes to the house of the Brahmin. He finds Monigo sleeping like a log on a settee, dressed in full regalia. His *khowal* hangs down his chest, the muroli clenched in the left fist resting on the settee.

"Come on sleepyhead, time to get up. Wake up, boy," Manu calls Monigo, shaking his body, but to little avail. Brinda's dance is almost over. Manu lifts Monigo with a mighty heave and carries him towards the rasomondoli. He lays the lad down on the bed decorated with flowers in the western side of the rasomondoli. Trying his best to wake him up, Manu perspires profusely. The whole world is wide awake on rasopurnima night except Sri Krishna—the main consort of Radha, with whom she has a tryst. Krishna lies in deep slumber. Manu makes repeated bids to wake him up. Hoba too throws a worried sidelong glance at Monigo while doing a twirl.

"All my efforts are in vain. Can anyone bring me some tamarind?" Manu shouts across. Tamarind arrives in a few moments and Monigo automatically opens his mouth, even in his sleep. The tamarind treat to his taste buds makes him grimace. He opens his eyes and blinks at the bright lights of the rasomondoli, rubbing off sleep from his eyes. Everybody heaves a sigh of relief.

"*Shoyatto aji e...e uthil Shyam ...m...m, nagoro Kalia...a...a* (The eternal lover boy Shyam Kalia rises from his bed)." The deep timbre of the patoli's voice rises above the babbling voices of the audience. Her vocal acrobatics keep the audience spellbound.

Lord Krishna gets up from the floral bed, rubbing his eyes. Holding the loose end of the dhoti with his left hand and spinning the muroli with the right he makes his grand entry to the sound of thunderous applause. Finally he makes a few dance moves and steps in with the beat of the mridongo. "*Kiba jhonjhon. Jhon nono-nono-nupuro bajaye, kiba jhonjhon...*"

The dance of Sri Krishna reaches its climax. He jumps and dances the length and breadth of the rasomondoli. The emotionally moved audience shower Monigo with *laddu*, *nokuldana* and *batasa,* littering the floor of the rasomondoli. Dressed in full regalia, Monigo tonight is Sri Krishna incarnate. His feet hardly touch the ground when he dances.

"Horibol, Horibol," the audience shouts aloud, bursting into tears. The transparent veil fails to hide Hoba's eyes filled with tears. Manu, sitting outside the rasomondoli with hands folded, is on the verge of tears too.

"*Dhin khere kheretang, kheretang, khit, ta gere gere dhei...*"

Turning a complete somersault, Lord Krishna stands on a *golisafita*[95] under the kadamba tree, made of green leafy branches, in the *tribhongo bhongi*[96]. A shower of flowers follows. With tears of divine love the audience rushes to Krishna and bows down. Sitting within the girth of her pollei, Hoba too extends her hands, holds the legs of the Lord and cries. Offering a few coins at the feet of Krishna, Manu also falls prostrate on the ground. He rolls on the ground, while tears stream down his cheeks. Oja Karna Singh rushes to the rasomondoli with hands raised high. Crying aloud, he too falls at the feet of Lord Krishna. Tears begin to flow from his eyes—like two melting glaciers.

Monigo is taken aback. What a bizarre scene! Why all the weeping and idol worship? Stunned, Monigo looks at the elders. Oja Guna bows down to him and starts crying, so does the audience. Monigo too bursts into tears, his emotions in a turmoil. Hoba

---

95 *Golisafita*: A colourful seat woven from cutpieces and strips of fabric.

96 *Tribhongo bhongi*: The typical standing posture of Krishna with head, waist and legs turned at a particular angle.

tries to console her son. Passions rise and many in the audience decide to spend and enjoy the night at the mandap.

"*Ginteinta khitta dheinta, ginteinta...*"

Bana is always upbeat and ready to go. At the loud and crisp sound of the mridongo she starts dancing with perfect hand movements and footwork. Dancing gracefully she makes her way into the rasomondoli, her pretty face under the beautiful muslin veil partly illuminated by the bright glow of lights. With Srimati Radha leading from the front, the gopis enter the rasomondoli. Sweet music fills the night air.

"*Dhin khere kheretang, kheretang, khit ta gere gere dhei.*" The dance rises to a crescendo.

"*Horibol, Horibol,*" the audience keep shouting. A shower of laddus, nokuldana and batasa resumes. Dancing the night away, Radha finally closes up to Krishna and takes her position by him. The live Radha-Krishna pairing is complete. The audience rushes to bow down to the divine pair. Hoba comes out of the circular line of the *gopis* and bows down to the 'live-and-divine' duo. Monigo does not feel ill-at-ease tonight as Bana stands close to him, completing the perfect image of the divine couple. In fact he stands with the hint of a smile on his lips, his head inclined towards Bana. Two gopis start dancing and fanning the 'divine' couple. Other gopis surround them and start dancing and singing divine songs.

Gradually, Bana's head droops on to Monigo's left shoulder but a sleepy Monigo – tired and stiff from standing in a pose for a long while and his eyes heavy-lidded – doesn't shove Bana away! With a small smile Bana's mother approaches the divine pair. Monigo's father follows suit.

The Rasolila comes to an end with prayers for the divine couple. The audience as well as the gopis and the ojas return home, the air filled with the jingle jangle of the tinkling anklets of *brojogopis*. They praise the Rasolila in no uncertain terms!

"Brinda has elevated this rendition to a great height. And the sacrosanct chemistry between Radha and Krishna has infused rare emotion into the entire recital. Each of them has met one's match in the other," says one.

"The dance of Krishna isn't something to be forgotten soon. As though, God Himself came down to Nikunjavan at Vrindavan for the Rasolila."

However, dancing the night away, 'God' himself is fast asleep, on his way back home. Yes, fast asleep in full regalia, stretched across Manu's back. His right palm holds no muroli!

CHOUDHURY GOLAPCHAN

Golapchan at Viratsabha

*R*ajargaon *srimandap*. The Viratsabha is underway. The congregation has representatives from Tripura, Bhanugachh, Sylhet, Baromuni, Meherpur, Bikrampur, Hingla and Pratapgarh. It's a grand affair of the community.

Dhansena and Golapchan enter the *mandap*. With no room left in the front side of the mandap, they move to the rear where their friends sit. 'Blue-blooded' Dhansena basks in the glory of family heritage at such congregations. His friends treat him with respect, though they don't utter anything openly. They make room for him in the front row and Dhansena sits down with a flourish, his chest puffed up with pride. Somewhat overcoming his natural diffidence, his friend Golapchan makes room for himself behind Dhansena and steals a glance at his friends. All are dressed befitting the special occasion. Golapchan's Sunday best comprises a handloom-spun cotton shirt woven by his mother and a pair of green shorts—his regular school uniform. For him special dresses for special occasions are a luxury which his mother can ill afford.

Golapchan runs his eyes over the congregation. The dais on the west was decorated with a fresh clean snow-white cloth. The president, the chief guest and a few dignitaries were seated on the grand dais. The president rested his elbow on a fluffy cusion and sat half-inclined while presiding over the meeting, resembling Lord Bishnu in His *anantashayan*. Clad in crisp white dhoti-kurta, the president – a man of repute – was curly-haired and clean shaven, gifted with a clear complexion and a well-built body. Golapsena had only heard his name; he set his eyes on him for the first time today. Was an introduction necessary? His was a well known face among both young and old as well as in the Pancha Bishnupriyas. Golapchan glances at those sitting in the south. Brahmins, Rajkumars, pundits and others from all the porgonas sat in conformity with the Bishnupriya Manipuri mandap protocol. Those from the fairer sex sat in the north. Right from near the dais, the mandap was packed with scholars and people from the Bishnupriya Manipuri community who thronged the enclosure.

President Oja Sanatan rises from his anantashayan. In fact, the eloquent speech to be delivered by the oja has attracted the sea of people. Cleaning his golden spectacles with soft fabric, he puts his glasses on, lets the edge of his dhoti free, bows to the congregation and addresses the gathering:

"All the divine people, Brahmarsi, Rajarsi, the learned and Kshatriyas—true descendents of the Suryabongsha and Chandrabongsha..."

Golapchan looks at the ladies' enclosure. A smiling Brahmin woman, tired of kitchen and cooking, has her eyes fixed on her husband Yogeswar Mukherjee, seated in the front row on the south side of the mandap with thick sandal paste marks on his forehead and nose. Golapchan steals a glance at Dhansena. His friend's eyes are stuck on the gold chain adorning his father, Dhananjoy Rajkumar. The turbaned royal scion sits in his royal seat. The royal gold chain is said to be the prized possession of Kalaraja of Manipur. The family heirloom has been handed to Dhananjoy Rajkumar down a long genealogical tree of inheritance.

Golapchan releases a deep sigh. He has been deprived of paternal love since he was an infant and been raised by his mother in the house of his maternal uncle Kalachan, forced to take on his uncle's identity. Kalachan doesn't attend such meetings, neither does his mother. Golapchan's mother sits in the market, selling puffed rice and parched paddy displayed in a bamboo basket. He hangs his head down for a while before looking up again at the congregation. The crowd admiringly looks at Oja Sonatan – historian, linguist, litterateur and social worker – an all-in-one genius. Among those who listen to the lilting speech of Oja Sonatan on the identity of the Pancha Bishnupriyas with rapt attention are Eiga Jogeswar, Dhananjay Rajkumar, Brajakishore uncle, and the likes of Haren-da and Birmangal-da. Jogeswar has had to sell the cow he had received as a gift to give a treat to his expecting daughter at Meherpur; Dhananjay Rajkumar was a TB patient who couldn't afford expensive medical treatment and medicines and has had to depend on herbal healing; Brajakishore uncle had to sell three *bigha*s of arable land to teacher Kamalakanta of Beelbari to get his son out on bail from the police lock-up. Haren-da and Birmangal-da have washed their hands off government jobs even after paying hefty amounts as bribes. Golapchan is overwhelmed by the mesmerising words delivered in slow and measured cadence. "Brahmarshis, Rajarshis gathered here!" This isn't Rajargaon *srimandap*. This is truly and indeed, Hastinapur! The lilting voice of the venerable Oja Sonatan echoes around.

"We are a force to reckon with. We're descendents of Arjuna, the third Pandava. Babhrubahan was the son of Arjuna and princess Chitrangada. It was Babhrubahan who had brought the idol of Lord Bishnu armed with the *shankha* (the conchshell), the chakra (a spinning disc-like weapon with 108 serrated edges), *goda* (mace) and *padma* (lotus in full bloom) from Hastinapur, and installed them at Bishnupur in Manipur. The son of Babhrubahan is Dattamuni and his son is Liklaikhomba...and their heir is Kalaraja. The direct descendents of Kalaraja are the shining stars of our community. They are Dhananjoy Rajkumar and his cousins."

The audience breaks into rapturous applause.

The congregation turns towards Dhananjay Rajkumar. He's totally bewitched by the special attention given to him. His son Dhansena is also the centre of attraction among his peers. With eyes closed and a subtle smile playing around his lips, he listens intently to the speech.

Oja Sonatan has hooked the penury-stricken, illiterate community afflicted with an identity crisis, with the ancient concept of Aryavarta, en route the *Mahabharata*. The congregation is basking in the newfound aura of its past glory and renewed sense of self identity. It's a sweet, honey-layered dream casting a bleary effect on their vision.

The grand conclave concludes before dusk. All in the gathering are on their way back home, their faces glowing with 'Kshatriya splendour' and the blood of Arjuna boiling in their veins. Dhansena has to stay back to take home his ailing father. Golapchan, on the other hand, leaves for the market in a tearing hurry to meet his mother and take her home.

Melody magic along the Longai

Late at night, Golapchan and his mother are on their way back home from the market, ambling along the side of the Longai. With a bag in one hand and holding on to an indigenous oil-lit torch burning on a bamboo pole, Golapchan leads from the front. His mother Imashou follows him with a bamboo basket pressed against her waist. An unfurled headgear fashioned out of Manipuri *khuttei* – the colourful handwoven towel which is a trademark of sorts for a Bishnupriya Manipuri and his household – rests in the empty basket. The yellow beams of the oil torch gleam on the waters of Longai. The river smiles and throws back a fistful of dreams to light up their faces, as if to reciprocate.

Imashou hums a melodious number—"*O obhujhmon naa chinle tore...*(O restless mind, you have failed to know yourself)." Golapchan keeps silent. After singing a few lines, Imashou asks: "What's wrong with you? Why don't you sing with me?"

Golapchan sings the two lines along with his mother and falls silent once again. He's in no mood to sing any song today.

With Imashou completing the song solo, Golapsena asks her: "Ima, is it true that we're descendants of Arjuna, and our forefather is Brabhrubahana?"

"Certainly we are. He was the son of Chitrangada. Were these said at the Viratsabha?"

"Yes, Ima."

"What else was discussed?"

"Our language has evolved from Sanskrit through Shouraseni, not through Magadhi as is the case with the Mayangs near us," an impressed Golapchan says.

"Who said this?"

"Oja Sonatan. He delivered an impressive speech, stirring up my emotions when he addressed the audience as Brahmarshi and Rajarshi," says Golapchan.

"What's Shouraseni?" she asks her son.

"It's the Hindi spoken in North India," he replies.

"Oh I see. It's the language spoken at pilgrim centres. He could be right," she says.

"Ima, why is our clan called Raja Lokei? Are we descendents of the king like Rajkumars?"

"Could be."

"If so, why are there no royal seats for us near the Brahmins in the Viratsabha?"

"I don't know, my boy. What will you do with information regarding Raja Lokei and the descendents of Arjuna? We toil to make both ends meet."

"Even then, we need an identity of our own," says the son.

"Monigo, forget all that and just concentrate on your studies. Being an intelligent student, the entire village expects much from you, mind you! Make it a point that Dada too expects much from you. Won't you top the result sheet this year as well?"

The mention of his maternal uncle silences Golapchan abruptly. With his eyes on the waters of the Longai, he keeps walking fast. Imashou has to divert the topic.

"Fortune will smile on us only when you get a good job after completion of your college studies. Monigo, you will have to take me to your office when you sit as an office babu on a chair."

"No, I won't. I feel awkward," Golapchan breaks his silence. "I'm sure in the office you won't maintain any decorum but start talking loudly in our mother tongue. You won't even hesitate to sing a song there," he complains.

"What's there to be ashamed about if you speak your own mother tongue? Okay, I won't talk nor sing. I will only keep looking at you while sitting in a corner of the office."

Comrade Kalachan's equation

After his routine evening study and supper, Golapchan goes to bed. Imashou starts parching paddy. A sleepless Golapchan stares at the thatched roof of the house. It is a two-shed low-roof cottage. The main horizontal bar in the frame overhead can be reached when one stands on a cot. The roof of the house is his, but the very land where the house stands is his maternal uncle's. The house has been erected in a corner of the residential plot of Kalachan. Imashou and her son live an austere life in a separate house, with limited means. Maternal uncle and nephew living under the same roof is taboo in this region and hence the separate houses for them. A revolutionary of repute Kalachan himself is penury-driven.

Golapchan wonders why they don't have any residential plot of their own in the village. Why don't they have any paternal kin in the village?

"Monigo, your mind is still full of the Viratsabha, the *Mahabharata*, Arjun, Raja Lokei and the like. Have a sound sleep. You have to wake up early tomorrow morning. Aargh! They're busy with the *Mahabharata* of Hastinapur while imminent and burning issues like starvation death, community cancer, bleak match-making prospects of the girls of Raja Lokei[97], have been pushed to the backburner.

"Did those sitting on the dais come to the meeting with their sons and daughters, brothers and other kin? The truth is that while immunising their wards against such ethnic bugs, they're out to spoil the children of the downtrodden. Don't you know what Dada will think if he comes to know that you attend such meetings and waste your time?"

"Ima, why doesn't Mama attend such meetings?"

"He's ailing. In his prime, he was a great brawny brute of a man. The killer disease he's suffering from is a gift from prison. He's confined to bed. Otherwise..."

"Why doesn't uncle value caste, heredity and the like?"

"He is a communist and believes in equality. He believes that a man is rated by his deeds, not by his heredity. Right?"

---

97 Raja Lokei: Royal clan.

"Yes, right," the boy said. His Mama was a prisoner of his own conscience for having led the Pratapgarh revolution from the front. His disease had its roots in the third-degree torture that he had to suffer in prison. With no hope left for his cure, it was only a matter of time! Party cadres and leaders frequented his home.

Golapchan rates his uncle highly. He feels proud of him, but that doesn't essentially mean that he needs no identity of his own. Why don't people recognise him when he identifies himself as the son of Huru? Which village did his father actually hail from? What led him to stay in the residential plot of his in-laws?

"Ima, which village did my father hail from? Didn't he have any siblings?"

Imashou jumps in fright and stops stirring the bowl of sand that she is heating in a cauldron. She is scared of an impending storm. What a signal could this be? She diverts the topic, as usual:

"Monigo, haven't you slept as yet? Headache? Should I blend together mustard oil and the water from the hubble-bubble, and rub on your head? Don't forget to fetch a bucketful of sand from the riverbed tomorrow."

Imashou adds a bowlful of paddy in the hot sand in the cauldron for parching. With the paddy seeds popping constantly, the queries raised by Golapchan go unheard. He does not utter a word but ponders silently. As and when he raises queries on his father or his whereabouts, all his Ima does is divert the topic.

Next day Golapchan steps out of the house briefly after his morning spell of study.

"Monigo, come here," his uncle beckons him from inside the house.

Golapchan waits near the door. Kalachan sits on his cot inside the mosquito curtain, coughing. He's a TB patient. Apprehensive of the disease being transmitted to his nephew, he doesn't allow the lad to come near him. Though the prolonged confinement to bed has curled up the six-foot-tall man, the depth of his voice and the glow of his eyes are not all lost.

"Monigo, have you followed the lesson you have just read? The word stratification has been derived from the word stratum, meaning a class. Social classes – rich and poor, upper and lower, kings and subjects and their like – are all man-made. The day isn't far when everybody will line up under one equation, at the same level."

Golapchan quietly listens to his uncle with unwavering attention.

"History is the past. Right analysis of experiences gained from the past, using history in the context of the present-day situation and their right application so as to make right strides in the future is the maxim of development. Out of sheer admiration, if you walk forward looking back, you will miss the rhythm and fall. If you walk back, you will miss the civilisation bus. Am I clear? Alright! Now, go and practise arithmetic."

Nodding his head, Monigo leaves and wonders—

"Arithmetic! What arithmatic has uncle asked me to do? Why has he told me all this? Ima might have informed him of my presence at the Viratsabha yesterday. But I didn't see Ima going to uncle this morning! My uncle can certainly gather information lying in bed all the while!

Choudhury Golapchan's diary

After his routine study at night, Golapchan goes to bed. Imashou is still parching paddy. Golapchan doesn't know when his mother goes to bed. In the mornings he can hear his mother singing devotional songs for awakening Radha-Krishna before Golapchan actually wakes up and leaves the bed. He sighs deeply. He's no longer a child and realises the staggering load his mother bears, but he is quite helpless himself, to be able to help her out. All such unremittingly severe and brute realities of life make him toss and turn in bed. His sleepless eyes stare at the weed-covered roof above.

"Aunt Imashou, are you at home?" calls out a voice.

"Who's there? Oh, is it Nemai? Come in please, and sit down."

Golapchan peeps from inside the mosquito curtain. A man of about forty, clad in dhoti-punjabi, enters their house, leaning forward. He is Rakhal Rajkumar, a party cadre whom the lad has seen many a time before. Imashou and Kalachan fondly call him Nemai. Golapchan's father tied the knot with Imashou while staying in his house. Nemai sits on a low-floor stool near the hearth. Imashou serves him popped rice with a lump of molasses in a clean brass bowl. Eating the crispy snack, he asks Imashou:

"Where is the child?"

"You mean Monigo? He's sleeping. It's too late now. He's no longer a child. He has grown up."

"I heard Kalachan uncle isn't doing well. I've just come to enquire about his health and to get some tips on party matters."

"Where do you live now?"

"At Deochhara. With the death of MLA Goyaprasad, a by-election is imminent in that region. I am burdened with party work as a result."

The word Deochhara frightens Imachou out of her wits. The fear gets her adrenaline flowing. Shading the oil lamp with her hand, she stares at Golapchan for a while. To be doubly sure, she carries the lamp to her son's bed and ascertains that he's fast asleep. The bowl of paddy left in the hot cauldron has stopped popping. Nemai sits in the dark. Golapchan pretends to be fast asleep, playing possum. Assured that her son is sleeping, Imashou whispers to Nemai: "Is the landed property of Monigo's grandfather still intact? Do you get to see the property?"

Golapchan's strains his ears to catch every word.

"The abandoned nine-*bigha* plot on the edge of the village is still known as that of Choudhury Borkham Singh. Our Huru uncle's father was indeed a landlord."

"Hush! Speak softly! The boy will wake up," Imashou cautions Nemai.

"People say that Choudhury Borkham Singh had eight *dhuns*, that is 128 bighas of land at Tilthoi Bazaar, Ramnagar Camp and Deochhara. The popular story goes that a killer cholera struck the village. Deaths were the order of the day and that led Borkhom Singh's eldest daughter Patali to leave the village for Pratapgarh on a white horse so as to save her only brother, Huru. It's said that she took a sackful of gold and silver along with her. They, however, never went back to their village. What followed was a bloodbath. Encroachment on Choudhury Borkhom Singh's land led to fierce clashes that claimed as many as four lives, on the spot."

"That's why I've kept Monigo ignorant of all this. I'm ready to suffer, but won't let my only son live life on the edge of a precipice," Imashou whispers with conviction.

"Do the people there know that Patali Gidei was on your plot with her younger brother?" she asks Nemai.

"No. In fact, nobody there knows that I'm from Pratapgarh. In Tripura, I'm known as Rakhal Rajkumar. Nemai is an unknown name there."

Imashou heaves a sigh of relief.

"Has the residential plot too been encroached upon? It was believed to be a haunted one," Imashou says.

"With men haunting them, spirits have left for good. People have erected thatched houses in one corner of the plot. In spite of that, the plot looks empty and abandoned. The mango and jackfruit groves are still there of course. Auntie, had uncle never been there?"

"He had been there in the guise of a garment salesman but kept me in the dark about what happened after his return. The lawyer told us that since the land had been mutated in Monigo's father's name, the property could be regained if the encroachers were dragged to the court. Your uncle, however, rejected the advice outright. I am not sure why."

Eavesdropping on the whispered exchanges between his mother and Nemai, Golapchan is taken aback. He puts one hand close to his chest—his heart seems to be beating fast! And his eyelids fail to close for the night. He isn't one among the last dregs of society. Choudhury Borkham Singh's grandson couldn't be a vagabond. In fact, he was a landlord!

Next morning, Golapchan's body language speaks of a sudden change. Sitting down to study after his morning prayers, he gets lost in deep thought. He looks out of the window and lets his eyes wander across the blue and limitless sky. He is used to seeing the sky through the window only as a rag torn out of his old school shirt. Why was the sky always so gloomy?

In the morning, a flock of egrets flap their wings and fly away, the golden sunlight gleaming in their wings and the reflected glow enveloping the field like a canopy.

Golapchan hastily takes out his diary and puts down – 'Choudhury Golapchan' – on the cover, on the first page, on page two and at every space left to be written.

He then goes out, takes out his uncle's buffalo bull from its shed and leaves for the grazing ground along the rear canal. He reaches the grazing ground through a big ridge and alights from the bull with a big leap. Dhansena and the rest of his friends had been playing in the field.

Watching his regal style of alighting from the bull, Dhansena says: "What's the matter? You look as though you have alighted from a horse and not a bull?"

Letting the bull amble down to the grazing field, Golapchan says: "It's a horse indeed. A white horse!"

"Are you all right? You're calling a black bull a white horse!"

"Controlled by a skilled rider, a buffalo bull can run as fast as a horse. Our forefathers were fond of horse-riding by birth, you know?"

Golapchan isn't the same timid boy today. His words and body language speak of a devil-may-care attitude.

Imashou's darling goes missing

Imashou is restless. The sun is about to sink, but her Monigo hasn't returned from school as yet. He is never late from school! Imashou is already late for the market. Keeping the meal for Golapchan ready and covered with a bamboo basket, she closes the door and leaves for the market.

She doesn't find her son in the market too. Imashou lights her oil lamp and while buyers come and go her eyes continue to scan the market, but to no avail. Her son is nowhere to be seen. She grows impatient and hurriedly wraps up her business. Selling the remaining parched paddy and puffed rice at throwaway prices to a wholesaler, she leaves for home. On her way back home, she asks everybody she meets about Golapchan.

Returning home, she pushes the door open only to discover that the meal for Golapchan has been lying untouched. Instead of entering the house, she rushes to Kalachan, and blurts out, "Dada, Monigo hasn't returned from school yet. He hasn't been to the market to fetch me."

"The buffalo bull has also returned home on its own. We have also been wondering..." Kalachan says.

Not getting much in the way of information from her brother, Imashou trembles in fear and sits down on the ground.

"Imashou, make an enquiry and ask his classmates. There may be meetings today," Kalachan says.

Imashou rushes to Dhansena's house only to discover that the boy is massaging his ailing father. She asks him: "Dhansena, where's Monigo?"

"Aunt Imashou, we went to school together. On our way back home I didn't find him. I thought he might have had gone to the market to fetch you," the boy says.

Imashou fails to hold her tears back and starts sobbing aloud. "Oh Monigo, my darling..."

She rushes back home like a lunatic, and Dhansena follows her. Soon the villagers crowed to their courtyard, asking Imashou and Dhansena about Golapchan. While some start a search with oil-lit torches, others are out with drums and cymbals, suspecting that the boy might have been possessed by spirits. Yet some others leave for the river to check for any floating body. Imashou's beloved Monigo isn't to be found anywhere.

"Dada, what's in store for me? Monigo has gone missing." Imashou lies crying miserably on the floor by her brother's bed. Kalachan sits on the bed inside the mosquito curtain with his chin resting on the knees. Dhansena stands with tearful eyes near Imashou, drawing Kalachan's attention. He asks the boy: "Have you seen him in school?"

"Yes uncle. We sat together in class, but on my way back home I didn't spot him."

"Have you noticed any change in him, his mood or words?"

"Yes uncle. I could discern that something was wrong with him. He sported a devil-may-care attitude."

"Do you remember what you talked about today?"

"He looked as if he was on the verge of losing his mental balance. He also called a buffalo bull a horse, to be precise, a white horse!"

Imashou stops crying and glances at her brother. The two siblings exchange meaningful looks.

*

It's night. Rakhal Rajkumar is at the Communist party office at Deochhara. Chaiko enters and reports: "Rakhal, a strange boy has come to meet you."

"A stange boy! At this hour?"

Rakhal goes out with a torch. The boy bows to him.

"My boy, who are you? Where have you come from?"

"I'm from Khalopar of Pratapgarh. I am the nephew of Comrade Kalachan.

"Are you the son of Aunt Imashou? You mean you are Monigo? You have grown up! What brings you here at this hour?"

"To meet you, Dada."

"But why? Why have you... come in, come in."

They make Golapchan sit on a chair and settle down.

"Chaiko-dada, can you recognise him? He's the nephew of Comrade Kalachan and son of Huru uncle."

"You mean Choudhury Borkhom Singh's..."

"Yes, don't speak loudly. Even walls have ears."

A nostalgic Chaiko hugs Golapchan and asks in a tearful voice, "My boy, what led you to this part of the world?"

"I'm here to see the land of my forefathers, to snatch it back from the encroachers."

"How do you know that?" Rakhal asks him.

"I overheard you conversation about my grandfather, Choudhury Borkhom Singh, with Ima."

Rakhal keeps quiet. Some time later, he has a quiet discussion with Chaiko outside the room. After a long while both of them come in.

"Have you informed your Ima of this visit to Deochhara?" Rakhal asks the boy.

Without making up stories, Golapchan hangs his head down. Rakhal and Chaiko start explaining the situation.

"My boy, don't keep your hopes alive for that property. That's no longer yours. Claiming that property now will lead to another bloodbath. Just forget it," says Chaiko.

"But then, despite having everything in the world why should we be vagabonds? Should my Ima, daughter-in-law of Choudhury Borkhom Singh, sell parched paddy in the market? I, grandson of Choudhury Borkhom Singh, have to hang my head down in shame among my friends at meetings and public congregations," Golapchan bursts out, soon breaking into tears.

Rakhal rubs the boy's tears, and says, "Monigo, don't be unreasonable. Choudhury Borkhom Singh earned this property by his own sweat and blood. He didn't inherit it from his parents. In course of time, the property has gone to others. You accept the struggle for existence and create your identity yourself, honourably. Don't use a leaf taken out of your family's history as your identity card. Imashou aunt sells parched paddy in the market and that is her struggle for existence. All struggles are great and respectable. Don't be ashamed of it; feel proud of what your mother is doing for you."

Rakhal-dada speaks exactly like Kalachan-mama, wonders Golapchan, remembering his uncle.

"Chaiko-dada, please arrange to take Monigo to your house for the night, before the arrival of party cadres for the meeting. Board him on a bus for Patharkandi tomorrow morning. Make sure that his identity isn't revealed here."

Chaiko leaves the party office, taking Golapchan along.

*

In the wee hours of the next day, Chaiko takes Golapchan to see the plot of his forefathers. He had made Golapchan realise the hard reality the previous night. Golapchan still wished to have a look at the plot of his forefathers, and hence this predawn visit.

It was a sizeable plot of nine bighas, with a mango and a jackfruit orchard. Though a few huts had sprung up at random, the plot still retained its beauty. Golapchan rubs the damp earth across his forehead like sandal paste, takes a lump of soil in his pocket and pays the ultimate respect to the land of his ancestors by lying prone on the ground, weeping silently into the earth.

Golapchan on way to school

It's a lonely evening. A listless Imashou is lying on the floor of her house without food or drink. She doesn't even feel like lighting the lamp, let alone going to the market. Pushing open the door gently Golapchan enters the house. Rat-a-tat-tat... The mild sound of the door makes Imashou jump up, only to see her beloved Monigo standing in the house. Out of rage and frustration she hits him on the head with the tip of her knuckle. "Do you get sadistic pleasure seeing me suffering? Where did you go?" She starts heating her son repeatedly.

"Stop it, stop it... Laughing, Golapchan continues to receive the punishment from his mother and hugs her tight. Her anger starts melting, flowing out like the turbulent Longai. "Oh God, my beloved Monigo is back," she repeats to herself.

The neighbours gather with the news of the arrival of the missing Golapchan.

"Imashou, has Monigo come?"

"Yes, Dada."

"Go, Dada is calling you. The ailing man had to spend a sleepless night only for you." Imashou literally pushes Golapchan into the house. He walks into the house with confidence and bows down to Kalachan from outside the mosquito curtain. Imashou takes a long look at her son who seems to have grown much in stature overnight.

"Monigo, did you go to Deochhara?"

Golapchan continues to stand without uttering a single word with his head hanging down.

"You could have met Nemai there. He might have taught you the right lesson. Chasing a spectral fire would only make you lose your way. Know your right way now. Go and take rest."

Golapchan returns home. The villagers too leave soon.

Slowly he takes out the lump of soil from his pocket and tells his mother: "Ima, this is the soil of our ancestral land, our home."

Imashou had never seen her father-in-law, let alone his residential plot of land. She was married to Huru away from home and later lived with her brother. She too, rubs some soil on her forehead.

"Monigo," she murmurs with folded hands. "This is the dust of your forefathers' feet. Keep it safe and sacred."

Wrapped in a clean piece of cloth provided by his mother, Golapchan puts away the lump of clay on the study table along with his books.

❊

Golapchan prepares to go to school the next day. He takes out his diary and slashes out the prefix 'Choudhury' from his name with the quill. Walking to school along the river, he meets Dhansena. Both of them are exuberant. "I heard of your return last night. Where had you been?" asked Dhansena.

Golapchan puts the matter aside with a light wave of his hand. Dhansena keeps silent for a moment.

"I won't go to school today," he declares. "There's a meeting at Beelbari, right now. Oja Sonatan will deliver his lecture today as well. Are you coming with me?"

"No," Golapchan replies quietly.

"If that's so, give my attendance proxy when the teacher calls my name!"

Golapchan shakes his head.

A stunned Dhansena stares at Golapchan. Today he doesn't seem to be his usual self!

Dhansena leaves for the Beelbari srimandap. Before reaching his school, Golapchan stops to listen to the enchanting voice of Oja Sonatan wafting across like a voice-over—"We're a force to reckon with...We're the true descendents of Arjuna. Babhrubahan was the scion of the third Pandava Dhananjay and Ima Chitrangada...

ACKNOWLEDGEMENTS

*R*amlal Sinha has tirelessly worked on the stories for the last three years. He nurtured the stories like his own creations. I owe a debt of gratitude to him for his efforts. With high gratitude, I remember and thank *Littérateur de renommée* Shri Nirmal Kanti Bhattacharjee for taking time out of his busy schedule and giving valuable suggestions. I would like to thank my editor Mohua Mitra and all the others at Niyogi Books who ultimately presented this gift to the readers. I'm grateful to the publishers— Mr. Bikash De Niyogi and Mrs. Tultul De Niyogi for having this book out. I also gratefully remember the constructive criticism by Mr. Kanishka Gupta. I thank Mr. Subhajit Bhadra, my dear student, who constantly encourages me to write new stories, critically reviews and translates my stories. Once again I thank my creative mentor Brojendra Kumar Sinha, who finally showed us the way to make this publication see the light of the day. I remember with gratitude my friends, colleagues and students of Tezpur University who encourage me in my literary endeavours. My successes and failures in all endeavours are equally shared by my wife Sunanda, daughter Ilina, son Tathagata and all my family members.